Snapshots: The New Canadian Fiction

SNAPSHOTS:
The New Canadian Fiction

EDITED BY KRISTINA RUSSELO

Published by Black Moss Press
2450 Byng Road, Windsor, Ontario, Canada
N8W 3E8.

Black Moss books are distributed in Canada
and the United States by Firefly Books, Ltd.,
250 Sparks Avenue, Willowdale, Ontario, Canada
M2H 2S4.
All orders should be directed there.

Financial assistance towards publication of this book was gratefully
received from the Canada Council and the Ontario Arts Council.

Cover art by Chris Hampel.

Canadian Cataloguing in Publication Data

Main entry under title:

Snapshots

ISBN 0-88753-256-X

1. Short stories, Canadian (English). 2. Canadian literature (English) — 20th century. I. Russelo, Kristina M.V., 1968-   .

PS8329.S64 1992   C813'.0108054   C92-090222-7
PR9197.32.s64 1992

Acknowledgements

Several of these stories have appeared previously in other publications. Byrna Barclay's "Linnea, My Twinflower" and "Seeing Double" appeared in *Fiddlehead*, and her story "After Twenty-five Years, Still Working it Out" appeared in *200% Cracked Wheat*. M.A.C. Farrant's "Last Campaign" appeared in *Industrial Sabotage*, her story "The Early Plastic Shrine" in *Rampike,* "childless" in *The Berkeley Horse*, and "Happy Birthday" in *Next Exit*. Cherie Geauvreau's "Charioteer" appeared in *Canadian Fiction Magazine*. J.A. Hamilton's story, "Hummingbird," appeared in her book, *Body Rain*, her story "Vermilion" in *Grain*. Robert Hilles' "Apollo" appeared in *Event*. Stuart Ross' "Clean Plates, Clean Plates" appeared in *What!* Kent Thompson's "Worship" was read on *Morningside*.

This book was inspired by Martin Waxman and made possible through Marty Gervais' trust. I am extremely grateful to them and to the authors for their enthusiastic support, which made this book such a delight to work on through the past months.

For Wayne,
and for my family,
with love.

The Photo Album: An Introduction

Moments of intensity, those things which make the most irrepressible memories. Snapshots. Pages of a photo album. Frames of an 8mm film. The new Canadian fiction.

These last few years, people have become obsessed with video cameras, with filming every moment of vacation, of their children growing up, of the important moments in their lives. The impulse to capture the things which stand out in our lives is nothing new, but our methods are changing. I found myself recently watching with my husband a two-minute clip of his grandparents' wedding, filmed over fifty years ago on 8mm film. Brief, silent, and moving at a slightly unnatural speed, it had a sudden, gripping effect on me. My own wedding, videotaped four years ago in full colour, runs for over an hour with all the filmed best wishes from friends and family at the reception, and somehow fails to touch me in quite the same way. I find myself turning consistently instead to things more brief, sudden, and more intense. Frozen images of loved ones in the photo albums, and the few flickering films of the past we usually keep in the closet of a spare bedroom.

I have resigned myself to being a conservative, sometimes backwards individual with an abnormally acute sense of nostalgia. So it would have been easy for me to conclude that my taste in Canadian literature, as in film, reflects that sense of nostalgia, to decide that these small, powerful short stories I have come to love were merely an evolution of an older style, such as Cendrars' travel poems — Blaise Cendrars, a Swiss poet of the early twentieth century who was one of the first writers to make use of the "postcard" technique, travel poems, each of which was intended as a record of a single moment. That conclusion, however, eludes me, in the face of the originality of the stories in this book. These stories, for the most part, have a directness lacking in Cendrars' poems, a concreteness, an immediacy not of place, as in Cendrars' works, but of people and events. There is a newness here, an exciting originality of tone and content, and of theme.

In school we are taught over and over again that the underlying theme of Canadian literature from its beginnings has always been survival. In the earlier years, no one cared enough to challenge or probe at that declaration, and by the time we reached university, it was pretty much a given that yes, this was what Canadian short fiction was all about. Margaret Atwood's messages had been taken to heart. At the centre of any survival, however, is the ability to adapt, and adaptation in our literature is what we are seeing today. As some Canadians fight to survive and to create a culture that somehow will reflect who they are, Canadian literature is changing, evolving and adapting along with them. Hence, *Snapshots: The New Canadian Fiction,* a timely testimony to the development of our literary identity. It may be that we simply haven't yet developed a novel culture, that for now, our questions are best framed in these deeply probing short stories. If such is the case, then I have it within me to hope we are a long time in reaching the answers, for in these stories I find tremendous strength, skill and insight.

Beverley Daurio takes us in hand in the first of five selections from *100 Times I Turned to the Window and Saw Your Reflection There,* seizes us immediately with her second person narration, and suddenly "you" are on a set of railway tracks frantically trying to untie a friend before the train approaches, thwarted by the unfathomable calm of her willingness to meet this fate. In Barbara Novak's "The World," we become lost with the narrator in an aimless sense of futility, out of touch with the swirl of everyday life around her, unable to effect any sense of herself upon her world. Stuart Ross grips the reader in his surreal story "Door" with a sense of desperation and frustration as a man finds himself irrevocably separated from a woman he can no longer even see.

Snapshots. Vivid, sudden stories, encapsulating single moments or events, thoughts and emotions. Weeks, years and lifetimes, also, held within the space of a few short paragraphs by a tone and perspective of a unifying centre. Epics, distilled to a simple purity where focus, and not length or detail, is the strength. These stories make up a series of frames in a film, or pages in a photo album, into which the authors have breathed life and dimension, where somehow characters are created and developed, complete with a sense of their past and future, all within the span of a few short paragraphs.

Kristina Russelo
Amherstburg
July, 1992.

Seeing Double

He is not you, he just looks like you. The first time I saw him, I didn't know he was your double. I thought he was you. The man who halved a breakfast bun exactly the way you do, curving his left hand around it and pressing on the slicing knife with two fingers, then counting and cupping the sugared walnuts, dividing them into two even portions, one for the person across the table I couldn't see for the palm frond and the other for himself, that man had your fine-boned fingers, and he talked with them the way you do too. He looked at me out of your slanted green eyes. I didn't interrupt what I thought was a client meeting, and strode on, into the lobby, then down the stairs to the conference room where I found you at a table, holding a place for me, my half of your cinnamon bun waiting.

The second time I saw him/you I was missing you in another city, counting the nights until I would see you again. On my way to Safeway to replace the candles we burned at both ends the nights we couldn't sleep on the road, we almost hit head on, your twin and I. The white car cutting around, in front of me was yours. The man driving it had your arched brow, its deep furrows, your brown hair swept back and curling up from the collar of your leather jacket. He looked at me out of your green eyes. I was afraid I would see myself navigating in the bucket seat beside him, unable to tell which cars were moving away or approaching, no connection between dots on the map, divided by words, yet connecting, your impossible profile caught in the sideview mirror.

There is a third and last time for everything. A weather watch at the window, I waited for you. Your car curving around the crescent. And there he was, on the other side of the street, striding the way you do, feet splayed out, his weight heavier on the left leg, the opposite of how you lean to the right, head swinging. Your leather jacket, hands thrust deep into the pockets. He turned left as you turned right. I knew I was safe as long as you never saw him. Another split second and you would have hit him head on.

And now, out of place in yet another city, I light a candle and leave it in your shadow. If you want nothing, need nothing of me, he will come to me, your double.

Linnaea, My Twinflower

Nothing could ever separate them. With her head on his shoulder, his right arm loosely around her, she always believed nothing — and no one — could ever come between them. She looked up at him, studied that perfect oval face, the round slope of his cheek curving down to the right angled jaw. With fingertip traced the wide arc of his lips. She tilted the tip of his nose up and he turned his head away from hers. In profile, the end of his nose pointed, his chin, he looked like a different man: thinner. The underfed look was what had made her want to take him home and feed him, no end to that. No end to the struggle, to the control she gave him and her fight to take it back. The separation and the division of goods, two of everything, came when he least expected it. They would never be the same again.

No one could tell them apart. Their hands were joined, one left one right, round intertwined leaves. On the ultrasound screen, they looked like evergreen twinflowers with long woody-stem legs, bell-shaped petal heads. Inseparable, even when that single egg divided in two and twinned its identical cells into even halves. They were lifted from their mother with right and left hands still clenched. They were twinflowers, with her dark hair and wide eyes, his large sensual mouth and cameo nose. The grandparents marvelled at the perfect combination, called them the monkeys, See and Do. No end to the tricks, the trouble doubled. Only the parents could tell them apart, though they said they didn't know how they did it. The firstborn exactly like her easy-going father, careful to watch both ways when crossing the street, led her sister by the hand. She was swifter with sums and dividing two groups of two. The secondborn exactly like her mother, at the top of the waterslide, daring her sister to go first, was quick to leap then look behind her. She was faster with words, but wanting to make the story better, she rubbed out too hard, with eraser shredded the paper, then tore it into two pieces. After the parents split.

After the story, she lies between them, with her head on her firstborn's shoulder, the second child asleep, left arm slung loosely across her stomach. She looks up at the daughter most like the father, that full face changed in profile, high brow furrowed now. His right angled jaw, the chin jutting, and in the slant of the child's blue-green eyes, she sees him.

    She calls to tell him how she knows them apart.

Getting Back, The Nights

She says she's found a way to get back the nights we didn't make love. She means to take them all back, the wine 'n dine nights she says I bolted from her, left her to burrow alone in the double bed, no comfort in the leftover Blue Nun. Get back at me, more like it. I'm supposed to take my shower and then see the surprise she's got for me. In the driveway. So I'm nervous as a half fucked fox and just as naked when I look out and see she's taken the rear window right out of the car. And I'm flying out, flapping my arms and yelling about breaking and entering, the trunk's hood rattling on its side on the lawn, and the backseat too. Well, fuck me gently, she's made a big soft bed in the back, her fluffy comforter and feathery pillows all puffed up, and she's cozy as can be, cooing too. She says she's put it right and we're going back, and I don't know how she does it but the car starts rolling, curving down, and I leap and jump in just in time, but the brakes fail, she's got it in cruise control, the car careening backwards. Going back to all the northern nights, lights dancing. The stars are aligned now, she says. And doesn't stop till we're halfway back, in the valley of our beginning, so she says, and I don't know where they come from, but women in blue all just like her, wave bangled arms, scarves. Cheering. A celebration of something better, she says. A close call. I'm out of the car, around the back, and I don't know how she does it, but she's got me diving in, right through the open back window, rolling and turning and wallowing with her till I'm all tangled up and feather tickled. She whispers she's found a way to take me back to all the unrequited nights. The rest is up to me.

After Twenty-five Years, Still Working It Out

Oh baby, he doesn't laugh like that when he's awake. Curled under the covers, he chuckles in his sleep, and it's making you crazy. When he slept on his back and snored you cured him by pinching his nose, and now you try everything, even pat his bum with a broom, but you can't stop his snuffling and snorting. His shoulders shake slightly as if he's sharing a secret under the sheet the way he did with you when he could stay awake long enough to romp. You've just got to know what's so funny. You lie still, hoping he'll talk in his sleep and give it away, but he never does.

He always told you everything, but every morning he says he can't remember his dreams. He says he's happy with you, that's all. But you're sure he dreams of a four-breasted woman who neighs, one with eight legs who can fly, or worse: someone you know. The fluffy secretary who makes up in hair what she lacks in height. The gas jockey who can't zip up her jacket. Or the girl with incurable giggles who slaps bums with the towels she hands out at the Y. You always said if he ever cheated you would know by the way he walked down the hall: all the leg action from the knees down.

You try to tickle him awake to catch him in the act, but that only makes him chortle louder. He sleeps with the sheet over his head. You slide out of bed, creep around to his side, kneel on the floor, carefully oh so slowly lift the sheet and stick your head under it. Nose to nose. His twitches. Ears wiggle, bottom lip wobbles, Adam's apple bobs, chuckle chuckle, chort. He has one grey hair on his chest. And then you know how you can stop him from having such a good time without you.

In his sleep you are laughing.

Markleson

His full name was Everett Lloyd Philip Markleson but on his office door, the black plaque read Prof. E.L.P. Markleson. *Professor* Markleson. All three of his given names had evaporated over the years. He was, of course, Professor Markleson. Professor Emeritus Markleson. Sometimes, as he sauntered down the beige hallway reading a newly arrived learned journal as he walked, Professor Markleson would accidentally open my door and walk in thinking it was his office. He would look at me briefly in complete bewilderment, decide I was clearly the one in error and ask me to leave *his* office. Out of deference to his scholarly reputation, I would vacate my own office, allow him to sit at my desk. He had never been a man of error and it was impossible for him to own up to fallibility. I would not return until I was certain Professor Markleson had gone off to teach a graduate seminar in semiotics to his class of three: a vivacious Pakistani woman, a gaunt pale Japanese scholar of almost indeterminate sex, and a thirty-year-old immigrant from Calcutta whose name sounded exactly like the words to a chant Allen Ginsburg had once lifted from the Hindus. Apparently, North Americans had little use for semiotics and the field had been turned over to the Asians.

Professor Markleson was world-renowned for his seminal work in the field of twentieth-century semiotics and he was, alas, the father of semiotic archeology as well. Even from the start the university heads were hard pressed as to which department was appropriate for a man in this field so it was settled to place him in the English department. Much of his respect had grown over the years because so few of the other professors even knew what semiotics was. Markleson had a noticeable speech defect and, before going off to Oxford, he had seen a stormy childhood in an outpost in Newfoundland where very little standard English had been spoken. Few of Markleson's colleagues could understand his potpourri of accents marbled by the defective palate. All of this served to heighten respect and regard for Markleson. He had political clout in the department and was, in fact, my advocate. If it wasn't for Markleson, I probably wouldn't have been hired.

Once a week he would invite me into *his* office. I was offered a seat in an ancient stuffed chair. Horsehair bristled through the upholstery and it smelled decidedly of cat piss. Markleson would conduct our conversation while darning socks or, on the odd occasion, grading a graduate essay on, say, mythopoetic semiologistics.

"Who teaches these people to write, anyway?" he once asked me, throwing down a twenty-pager concerning one of his less favourite subjects: literature. Obviously, we would have to have gone beyond the West to find an answer to his question. He forever spoke of undergraduate study as if it was, in fact, kindergarten. In the last two decades, the department had not suffered Professor Markleson to teach an undergraduate course.

Between our offices was a wall designed to function much like a megaphone. Markleson cleared his throat every twenty seconds with the enthusiasm of a man who enjoyed making noises. He enjoyed his own company best and spoke fluently to himself in Gaelic, German, Icelandic, Old English and what I presumed to be Esperanto. Like so many of us, he had become skillful at answering any question put to him by quoting another source. If I was likely to answer a student's query on metaphysics with a reference to T.S. Eliot, Markleson would instead refer the questioner to Hinklemeyer, Wimbells, Sneed or Riggs.

"I'm holding up five fingers, is that correct?"

"Yes," I answered, not having to count the digits.

"That's where you are wrong, my boy," he mumbled, then shared a good laugh with the wallpaper. These were the conversations we had. He treated me like a son, so I assumed the role of a well-bred, attentive and respectful step-son who knew his old man to be bonkers.

The Principal in the Pink Shirt

When things got boring in Rekjavik I decided to take a bus out of town to a small village whose name I couldn't pronounce. I had no good reason for going there except for the fact that it was January in Iceland and I was tired of hanging around the Salvation Army bunkhouse.

At the bus terminal everyone was drinking Pepsi Cola warm and the sun was lackadaisically making an 11:30 appearance outside. I sat reading a novel which is a really stupid thing to do when you are sitting in any foreign country but it quickly began to snow outside, erasing the already tardy sun and announcing the arrival of the tundra bus.

Outside the city limits there was nothing that looked at all like anything in particular. The bus driver, as far as I could figure, was inventing his own road across the snow-vanished nothing landscape.

The village appeared at the end of the invented road and I got off with a small clot of Icelanders who rushed to buy more warm soft drinks. Since I had no purpose in being in the village I went looking for something public and could only turn up a school. Schools were the reason I was in Iceland; I was tired of them.

Nonetheless there was noise there and I was dead tired of quiet, that is, late night Salvation Army quiet which involves steam heat noises and machine guns bursts of coughing. I felt compelled to hang out, however briefly, with younger people who weren't on the verge of dying.

A young woman greeted me with restraint but eventually invited me into a classroom where she began a music class. It was one of those universal sort of dances where in the end, everyone falls down. She shouted out orders with incredible volume and like a true North American I was overwhelmed with the degree of classroom discipline. It was also curious to see all age groups together from three-year-olds up to really big kids. Kindergarten through university from what I could tell.

Eventually I was shuttled to the principal's office where he asked in broken English why I was there. I explained that I was a substitute teacher back in Newark, New Jersey and it was good to see the lack of guns and knives in the hallways here.

He buttoned the button on the top of his pink shirt and indicated that I wasn't being understood; that his English was not very good and that I should keep going until I hit on something that fell into his vocabulary.

So I went from teaching to Newark to violence and eventually suggested the word "Kojak," which clicked and everything seemed to be okay after that. We nodded and smiled at each other the way people do when their tongues have been cut out and they want to be polite.

It was recess and the kids were outside heaving snowballs at each other which raised the ire of the principal. Without ado, he launched himself out the door and flung his pink-shirted form against the ivory white world. He smashed two heads together, although I'm sure there was love in it, and returned to resume our nodding conversation. The kids moved off behind a shed to continue their violence at all cost, the snow filled up the emptiness of Iceland and the sun was already in retreat from its brief token appearance.

Making Adjustments

Jacob Kobol got himself up out of bed and put a harness on his imagination. Good God, what a night. He was confounded by the things that sleep put into an old man's imagination. He had promised to stop thinking of himself as old but it was impossible. Sixty-five is not old. When he turned eighty, he re-informed himself, sixty-five will seem like adolescence. The truth was this: he wanted to be old but he was not allowed to be. Asleep, it was as if he had boarded a strange train and was in another man's body; a younger man's body. Nothing in his real life gave substance to the things that went on in his head while he slept. "You're a sex maniac," he chastised his image in the bedroom mirror, "and even worse than that. You should be shot, stoned, hanged by the neck until dead."

To wake up was to get off the train, always at the same station, it was to be alive again in his own skin and to be dead as well. Maybe he should go to a doctor, a therapist, a specialist in geriatrics, a counsellor, or some religious person whose profession it was to put Ajax to the soul. But he wasn't worried about his soul. He was more interested in the young man locked up in his own tired body, the young man who went crazy inside his imagination every night and sometimes started to make appearances in broad daylight among friends and acquaintances on the street or in people's homes. This young man could not possibly have been himself in any form because Jacob Kobol had never been a young man. He was a boy once for a very short time and then suddenly he was a man working his hands raw in a textile factory and then, overnight, he had become a very old man for whom doors opened quickly and who made money too easily.

When Ella died, he did two things. He stopped drinking coffee and he sold his carpeting company. He knew that he would think of Ella every time he drank coffee alone. It would kill him, so he stopped. And he knew he could not show up at the plant for his employees to feel sorry for him or try to be kind and helpful to a finicky old widower. Some things he knew he could not handle.

The Year 1972

I pay $95 a month for the room; the guy downstairs from the acid rock band pays a hundred. He has a bigger room with a ceiling painted flat black but I'm closer to the bathroom. My days are mostly made up of travelling around town looking for interesting things in people's trash. I've found dozens of old card tables, for example. All have exactly one faulty leg and a teastain caused by a lady who leaned too hard on that last fatal card game.

Once I found lots of teeth. There was a total of 1005 sets of plaster of Paris teeth waiting for the trashmen outside the home of a retiring orthodontist, but I took them all back to my room. The gums had all been painted pink by hand. I would like to have met the girl who painted all those gums pink.

I find stocks and bonds and old stringed instruments. Even found some booze once — a cheap bottle of apple brandy. I drank it and it was awful. Sleeping bags and tents. A 1912 vacuum cleaner that empties without paper inserts. How ingenious the ancients were! There is even a shooting star on the cloth bag that looks like something a Scotsman would use to make music. Trailing the shooting star are the words HAMILTON BEACH.

I have found everything in the trash of these suburban streets at least once. It's hard to believe but I'm directed to these things by God. I found roller skates but no key. Three houses down I found the key taped to a post card along with other thrown-away mail from the Depression.

Everything I find stays with me in my $95 room. A man moved in upstairs who painted houses for a living in the day and drank oral antiseptic in the night. The police came one night and took him back to prison in Raleigh, North Carolina. It was second degree murder, not first.

I read maps and outdated textbooks in the day and watch the children play outside the Montessori school next door. A birch tree grows outside my window. It turns blue in the evening just before the light is gone from the sky.

I've learned to cut old beer bottles turning them into drinking glasses and translate French essays concerning the history of the sonnet. One day I used my binoculars to watch people who walked by my house. This took three hours. The next three hours I looked at a teardrop beneath a microscope. The microscope and binoculars had both been found in the trash.

The Man With the Gift of Tongues

At a local community meeting where we discussed a local community problem there was a man who continually volunteered to translate the proceedings. After I spoke my little piece concerning the local community problem, he stood up and began, "I think what Lesley is trying to say is..." and he would proceed to clear up any misunderstandings I had concerning my ideas. He was happy to do the same for each and every speaker until by the end of the evening it was clear that we were all speaking difficult foreign languages and our ideas had to be corralled into neat little packages much in the same way that meat on the hoof is turned into frozen one pound squares of hamburger.

Watching With Father

It was summer. Inside I was watching George Chuvalo fight Muhammad Ali. Our television was a black and white. The picture was grainy and the sound bad. My father and I watched the fight in silence. I lay still on the carpet, looking up at the television, my palms sweating profusely. My father sat back on the couch, clenching and unclenching his fists. Between rounds he sipped from a beer.

Chuvalo received a full fifteen round beating, but he remained standing. He was proud and strong and — it seemed to me at the time — intensely Canadian: quiet, gracious, indomitable. I was proud. When it was over, my father shook his head in disbelief. "That man," he said, "is absolutely the slowest man ever to put on gloves." I bristled. I was thirteen years old and a living breathing antenna. I was possessed by the strangest convictions.

Following Along

for Thomas Wiloch

So I went along with them. Then another guy showed up and we all said come with us. We were all of us going and it was OK to be going along together, it was nice. Then someone else showed up but he was different from the rest of us guys. So we told him, do not follow us, don't come along, we don't like it. But he kept coming along with us, at our heels. We said to him again, to his face, don't come along with us, do not follow along. He stood still and we started up again and we thought he had finally gotten the message. We thought we had left him behind, and we felt good about that, me and the rest of the guys. Then we heard footsteps and it was him again and he was coming along with us again. We were all of us getting a funny feeling in our guts. I was starting to get scared thinking about what I was feeling and what I might do and then I looked at the others and they were also feeling the same way I was and I knew something was going to happen to the guy who was coming along with us even though we told him not to. What was going to happen to him was going to be horrible in the extreme. Then all of a sudden he stopped and said out loud, ahh fuck it, you're a bunch of stupid idiots and I don't care where you go. And he stopped and turned around and went running off in the opposite direction. After he had been gone a long time we stopped waiting for him to change his mind and return to us. So then we started up again going in the direction we had been going in all along.

City

Ah'med Khiruani decided one city to be fabulous for this reason: its streets formed a pattern of such demonic complexity that newcomers, once inside the city walls, wandered about for years trying to find a street leading out. During this time the travellers sought out a means to live, a place to live, a lover. They married and had children. They paid taxes. Eventually the travellers discovered themselves to be, in fact, residents who had no desire to leave; rather they prayed only to remain within the city walls till the day they died.

Selections from *100 Times I Turned to the Window and Saw Your Reflection There*

You live a couple of miles from here and have never seen a train go by, but it is still unnerving to be tied to the tracks. She has used long scarves, lengths of lace, and thin nylon ribbon. Her fingers are small, but strong and nimble; the knots she made were learned and practised; it will take her several minutes to untie you. The iron of the tracks is black and rusted, the ties are grey and dry, and there is a white gravel bed underneath. Your knees are slung over the bottom rail, and the back of your neck rests on the other, your head uncomfortably hanging down the metal ridge. The two of you are equally committed to what you are doing, however, and you do not complain. There are bits of grass in your hair, dust on your arm and on your yellow gingham skirt and black shoes. The sun is pleasantly warm as the knots come undone. A mild breeze pushes at the shrubs and small trees that line the right of way, where you keep watch for wild dogs. The grass has not been cut for a long time, and dried and dusty weeds catch in her skirt as she works at the lace knotted around your waist. At this point, something is over. There is no entertainment in undoing what you have done so far. When you are finally sitting up, your friend says, *All right then, it's my turn*, and you trade places. You shake your skirt and flip your hair to get the dirt out of it, then slowly begin to tie her to the tracks, winding lengths of rag and lace under the ties where the earth allows it, and around the rails under her knees and around her neck.

You have done this before. Trailing around the house, gathering materials, different every week, you ignore chains and electrical wire and extension cords for the softer items you like to feel around your knees and waists: a blue chambray rag, a cashmere scarf with soft fringes, a strip of fine yellow wool.

You hear the train at the same time. It is coming from the same direction as the wind, rumbling, and at first that's what you think it is, but the wind doesn't send ahead the smell of oily dust. Neither of you starts. You begin untying knots as rapidly as you can. Your hands do not shake. You take all advantage of your strong fingernails, and manage to tear the wool holding one of her legs to the iron. Gravel drives into your ankles and dry wood slivers press against your hip as you lean forward to untie your friend's neck. The train is visible, an approaching height, not terror yet. You work your fingers to free your friend's wrists. This makes sense. With her hands free, she may be able to force herself out of her supine position and walk away.

But she does not. She takes her free hands and grips you about the neck, tightly. She brings your face down to her chest. She is wasting time. You wriggle, force your knees hard into the dirt, against the rail, and pull back. Fingernails dig into the soft skin of your shoulders, and you are surprised to see your friend's calm face looking up at the sky as the train noise becomes real and present and the rush of its air can be felt on your skin. You work stupidly at the knots, you take your teeth down to the cloth and wrench her other knee free, you bite through the lace at her waist and rip that, too, feeling blood on your chin. The train is coming but she stays lying on the tracks looking up at the sky with a patient face. You slide backward down the embankment, you pull on her feet as the train slides by and leaves you holding something partial. The weeds move like the wind moves weeds, and you expect, touching her warm ankle with your fingers, you expect the ground to be shuddering, but it is not, because underneath it is knotted and knotted and knotted to itself, to the weeds, to the train.

***

You walk around the carnival spending the money you saved over several weeks of babysitting. The asphalt looks different, grimier, with cotton candy cones strewn about and fat electrical wires snaking from booth to machine. You tend to want to look under things: a glimpse of greasy gears here, an unshaven man in a ripped t-shirt behind the dingy glass there. You aren't the kind of girls to whom such a place is magical: it is Saturday afternoon, and you mean to spend it intensely.

You have skipped Greek in order to come because Betsy was on the point of tears about it on the phone. *You can catch up*, Betsy said, and now she stands cheerfully biting into two waffles with ice cream dripping out of them, surveying the machines that can spin you about, deciding which one you should try next. The body suspended in air, the constant knowledge that the machinery could seize and throw you back onto the cement or into one of the temporary metal fences that ring every ride. Betsy won't go up alone, but once there, she thinks nothing of almost tipping the seat by swinging back and forth, or sticking her arms straight up into the air when the small paper sign in front instructs riders to hold tightly onto the bar.

You throw darts at balloons for a while, confer about the lopsided weights in them, and finally win a stuffed bear which you promptly hand to a passing woman with a pram and a three-year-old in tow. Betsy eats chips from a greasy paper bag, and cotton candy, from which you freely take large bites. You hand in tickets for the haunted house — which scares you when the cart seems to jerk sideways — for the lagoon, and for the snaky jet. The rocket looks tame enough: a machine that spins on a level platform; but it goes very quickly, and when you get off, Betsy looks green. Betsy puts her hand on your arm, and you lead her around to the back of one of the false fronts. Betsy vomits again and again, with one hand holding onto a metal strut and one hand holding back her hair. She leans over away from your shoes and coughs.

If you were a boy, you say, looking past Betsy at the people grouped around the ring toss with the fuzzy snakes hanging down and the red awning that keeps the sun off, *if you were a boy I'd want to go out with you and we could get married. It's too bad.*

***

It is August, and around you in the tall grass live things chirp and rustle. You have been staying at your grandmother's house for more than a week. The red brick house is trimmed with carved wood that is painted white, and stands two hundred feet from the highway that leads south to Toronto. She warns you about the highway. Over and over again: the cars drive fast, but you run toward it anyway, toward the bright things that are moving, whenever no voice from the screen door pulls you back.

You don't know what day it is. You have been stung by a bee; you have helped to bake buttertarts with thick white pastry turned at the edges. In your pocket are what your grandmother calls the flower scissors; you dart from place to place with the wind in your hair, cutting blue cornflowers and queen anne's lace, the stems so much harder than those of the soft gladioli in the garden.

You are hiding near the road in a clump of grass, your white shorts digging into your thighs, when a car pulls over onto the shoulder of the highway. Its lights flick off, and the passenger door opens, but no one gets out; you see only a hand pulled back. The car looks familiar, and you stand and walk toward it, pushing grass out of the way with your scissors hand, the few flowers you have gathered in the other. At first you only see a shape, a head in profile, through the open door. Your sneakers hit gravel; the inside of the car is upholstered in red. It is your other grandmother in the car. An orange afghan your cousin knitted is folded on the front seat. She asks you how you are, hands you a package of spearmint gum, your favourite kind, and drives away.

***

You are sitting in a green metal chair. To your left, there are windows. None of the windows are open. In front of you is a large rectangle of white paper neatly covering the flat plastic surface of a desk that has been pushed together with seven other desks. Old juice tins filled with paint sit where the desks meet. Brush handles stick out of the tins. The girl sitting across from you is squinting at her paper. The girl sitting to your right has already made a tree. The tree has a brown trunk with drips leading up to it, a round green ball for a top, and reddish spots that are supposed to be apples turning brown in the green paint. The teacher said to paint the sky. You ask the girl across from you how to do the sun. She shrugs. To the right of her treetop, the other girl has made a yellow circle with thick yellow bars sticking out of it. This is a sun, and you paint one too, filling in the centre with yellow until the paper is so wet there are fuzzy paper bits floating in the paint. You work hard to cover the paper with colour. Your wrist wobbles. Green grass. A black house with square windows and pink curtains. You have painted in a second sun, which the teacher points out is incorrect. You let the extra sun dry and cover it with a big white cloud.

After recess, you stand with the others at the back of the classroom and hang your coat on a hook. You stamp your feet to warm them. The desks have been moved back into rows, and the paintings, the white paper curled and bumpy, have been stapled to bulletin boards that go as high as the ceiling and line the inside walls of the room. You look for your painting. You try to remember exactly how the paint went, on which side you painted the white cloud. You scan the dry papers with the beginning of panic, staring at thirty identical trees and houses and lawns and yellow suns.

***

You have never lived in this area and you have never been in this hospital before. It is a low, rectangular building set into the side of a hill. You release your seatbelt and step into the heat, stretching your legs after the long drive down through Tobermory and the Bruce Peninsula. You ask at the desk and are directed up the stairs, where you go looking down through the holes between the steps, your right hand lightly touching the iron railing. A fire door and two right turns.

She is lying in a white clean bed with chrome rails shining at the sides. The back of her head is on the pillow, her white hair very thin now, scalp showing through. Her lips are grey and chapped. You carefully remove the bits of kleenex by her cheek, announcing yourself to her softly. The room is unbearably hot, even with the curtains down, and you wonder why there are no fans, no flowers, why the unidentifiable red juice on the nightstand is in a styrofoam cup. She has had a stroke in the past day, and one eye droops while the other shines at you.

At this point, there is no entertainment in trying to undo the past for either of you. There is only the possibility of comfort.

Are you thirsty? you ask, taking up the spoon and cup, and she nods and opens her mouth a little. It's so hot. *I'll pull the bed up a bit first, if you like,* you tell her, and go to the crank at the bottom of the bed, turning the handle slowly, not enough to leave her sitting up.

She is paralysed on the left side. Her bad hand lies still and dry on her chest. You fill the spoon with juice and pour the liquid slowly, feeling through the steel how much she has taken. She swallows and swallows, her tongue keeping the liquid away from the parts of her mouth and throat where she can't feel, where it might choke her.

You have done this before, you suppose, only it was you propped in the chair, you with sweet happiness in your eyes, you whose little blue chambray suit was kept clean by a cloth tucked under your chin while you took food from a spoon.

Minutes go by. You see a little juice go down, you give water every few sips to clean the palate, you hold her good hand, tell her that you love her.

You both hear someone coming at the same time. The sound of voices comes from the hallway mixed with the rumble of a drug cart. You keep on with the juice, knowing that you will soon have to go. Your aunt is here, your cousins, and their sad and pleasant noise that you don't want to hear, although you nod and say hello.

Your aunt takes the cup from you, the spoon, your seat beside the bed. You lean down and hear her whisper before you stand away. You watch your aunt pour a full spoonful flat into the middle of her parched grey mouth, watch her cough and push the spoon away with her good hand.

No one has brought a fan. There is hot still air against your face and hers. You say something you won't remember to your aunt, knowing she has been at the bedside all along, while you were not. Nothing moves as the drug cart slides by outside the door, and you expect, remembering the touch of her warm good hand, you expect to be shuddering, but you are not, because underneath it is knotted and knotted to itself, to the heat, to the day.

Looking Down

On Sunday evening I took Ginger for her usual walk. It was the first really cold day of fall and I put on my overcoat and scarf. The street was dark and the trees rattled their branches in the wind. Ginger strained at the leash; she never had been trained properly. Underfoot were the crushed shells of chestnuts.

At the corner Ginger paused to sniff a sign pole. The wind picked up and flapped the bottom of my overcoat and I remembered how, as a child, I had wanted so badly to fly. At night, in bed, I had actually thought about this problem and the degree of mental concentration that flying would demand. Ginger was rooting around the pole and so I closed my eyes and concentrated now, stiffening my muscles. I felt myself rising; the toes of my Oxfords left the ground.

When I opened my eyes Ginger was looking at me from below, her head tilted to one side. I let go of the leash and rose another five feet or so. My overcoat filled with wind. Although it didn't seem necessary, I stretched out my arms as I had imagined as a child. My hands brushed the branches of the trees as I went up.

From this height the street looked regular and silent, rows of dark lawns and roofs. I thought hard and turned my body, rising higher and feeling the wind — colder up here — against my skin. I passed over several blocks before realising where I was headed.

Here the houses were smaller, in crescents and dead ends. Quite suddenly, it seemed, I was over the house where I grew up. The narrow drive, the back yard with a mulberry bush inside the fence. I drifted slowly up the street until I came to the elementary school. It was part brick, part block, with a sandy lot in the back. Despite the hour a boy was standing in the lot, near the back door. His short baseball jacket flapped against his loose shirt. A car pulled into the lot, an old Buick, crunching the gravel under the tires, and then a man in a suit got out. He walked towards the boy. And then I knew the boy was me. I'd been caught cheating and my father had been called from the office. Down below the man took the boy's hand and turned it over. I couldn't see from up here, but I knew that the palm was ink-smeared. The man — my father — didn't say anything. Just put his hand on the boy's shoulder and walked him back to the car.

I veered away. Over the candy store, the *schul*, the public pool. Flying was just as tiring as I had imagined it as a boy. The sky was lightening in the distance as I slowed and began to sink. It took what seemed my last energy to come down softly, on the souls of my shoes.

Ginger was waiting for me on the porch, curled up and shivering on the mat. Inside, I turned on the kitchen light, hung up my overcoat, and put on the kettle. No one else would get up for hours yet. I would make breakfast for them. My father had liked making us breakfast too. He was an early riser.

Line

I am standing in line to see a showing of *The Golden Age of Second Avenue*. When I pay for my ticket the woman can't find enough change. She has silver hair, pearl earrings and wears a sweater tight as a young girl's. A volunteer. This is obvious. The line in the narrow hall is already long. The first film began late. No one seems to know why. The line is getting restless. Voices rise. More gather behind me. A woman in a fur collar says, "I'm collecting Raoul Wallenberg books." A man wearing a yarmulke tilted on his scalp paces back and forth. He has a drooping eye and clutches a plastic box. "Rabbi, Rabbi!" He is in charge of the candy table. He shakes the box which is full of coins and asks if anyone wants to buy candy. The line just grows louder. The rabbi calls attention and begins a long explanation of why the second film is starting late. By the time the line realises he is saying something of importance and hushes down he has finished his speech. He coughs and makes a little bow. For the first time I begin to understand Kafka. Two young girls are talking in front of me. The one with wire-frame glasses and buck teeth keeps using the word "fascist." I feel old. She says, "Sometimes I just feel like chucking everything and going out to help some people." I want to laugh but if I do she won't understand. She won't understand that I love her. The film is narrated by Herschel Bernardi. His mother and father were actors in the Yiddish theatre.

Here In New York

A letter from M.:

"When are you going to join me here? There is nothing for you back home while here you can be free. Your family, bless them, are stifling you. And yet you believe that you have a duty to live for them rather than yourself.

"Let me describe my arrival a month ago. I took a cab in from La Guardia airport to Manhattan and what I saw was a vision: a skyline of dark towers and a million shining lights. The bridges spanning the East River were poems. Other cars swarmed around us as we drove and I felt a rhythm, a pulse, like a heart beat. On every corner a party was in progress. Hundreds of people laughing, running, selling, or buying, little jazz groups on the corners of lower Broadway, crowds streaming out of the theatres. I told the driver to go past Carnegie Hall and made him stop while I (I swear this is true) kissed the brick front.

"Already I have a life here; if I came back now I'd be lost. All day I practice. My teacher is Russian and brilliant. He cares about me as if I were his son. Often we dine together and he regales me with hilarious and touching stories about his career. To him the piano is not a mere instrument but the divine voice.

"It's true I'm so poor I hardly have two cents to rub together. But love — and sex — is free and I must only remind myself to be careful. The men here are beautiful and I suppose the women are too. But even with so little money we manage to hear concerts, sit late in restaurants, argue over books and films. We live joyfully and for now. Here in New York I'm part of the city, I belong. What would I do without Canal Street, the Forty-Second Street Library, the waffles at Sandolino's?

"In one week you'll know more people in New York than you've met in your whole life at home. You have no ambitions like I do? Fine. I've got a friend with a Ph.D. in philosophy who works as a bartender and spends his days reading Schopenhauer. Besides, in New York you'll discover your real vocation: it will come to you as a revelation. I can think of a dozen people you could share an apartment with. What am I saying? You'll live with me. Write back a single word: *yes*. It will change your whole life."

This letter arrived a year ago. I hesitated a long time in replying, and before I did M. returned home. He has given up the piano and works in the family medical-supply business. Since his return I haven't phoned him or returned his calls. But sometimes I pretend that his letter has just arrived, that I have taken out a sheet of paper, and that I am about to send my answer.

Buying the Newspaper

1

Walking down the street to buy the newspaper. Wondering at this 'permanent' world we build, of brick and stone and metal and ordered angles and curves.

2

Between the walls our lives flutter as erratically as animals banging in cages, exhausting themselves.

3

Waiting to cross the street. A car drives slowly by, as if looking for something lost. The change slides into the box.

4

There is a separation between the individual and the pavement underfoot that is unbearable to contemplate.

5

Tonight the city is the colour of a rose. Why does it make the heart break? An act of devotion: tucking the newspaper under the arm.

Cartoon

One day Fischer, eating lunch at his desk, was startled by a cartoon in the latest issue of a magazine.

The cartoonist was one of those notetakers to contemporary manners whom Fischer rarely found amusing, but this cartoon perfectly captured the nature of his affair with D. The failure of this relationship, during which marriage had been seriously discussed, had tormented Fischer for a month now. He suffered not only from the loss, but also because he blamed himself for mishandling a crucial moment. One evening Fischer had deliberately brought things to a head in order to tell D. everything that was wrong and yet at the same time to speak unguardedly of how he felt about her. But these complex feelings had come out as a kind of whine, and he had succeeded only in giving D. a chance to break it off.

And here was this cartoon, so astonishingly true to his experience with D., to everything that had been hopeful and absurd about it. He reached for a ruler to tear it from the page. Then he folded the cartoon and slipped it into his wallet.

Over the next few days Fischer became possessed by the idea of showing the cartoon to D. While he couldn't phone her or show up at her apartment door or even send it in a letter, he was bound to run into her some time. What he expected of this encounter he wasn't sure, only that the cartoon would make everything he had meant to say clear to her. But he didn't run into D. — not in a week or a month or three months. He relapsed into bachelorhood and slowly learned again how to enjoy the single, uncompromised life.

And then of course he saw her. She was standing on Bloor Street, looking confused for a moment, as if she had forgotten where she was going. Fischer said her name aloud before he knew what he was doing. The two exchanged pleasantries for a few moments and then D., glancing at her watch, excused herself. He didn't remember the cartoon until she was halfway across Bloor Street and by then it was too late. He merely watched her turn a corner and the meeting he'd been anticipating for almost a year was over.

His own lunch hour was almost up but he couldn't bear the thought of immediately returning, so he ducked into one of those new, sterile chain-cafés that seemed to be taking over the city. He sat down by the window and took the cartoon from his wallet, worn from all those months in his back pocket. Somehow it wasn't quite what he remembered, as if the characters had changed their expressions or the words had rearranged themselves. Had it never had anything to do with his affair with D., or had he forgotten what they had been like together? Looking at it now, he started to weep. An awful, physically painful weeping.

Without looking up, Fischer thought: if only D. would walk by and see me. But the only person who noticed him was one of the secretaries from the office. And she thought: good, you bastard, you suffer for a change. Flushed and trembling, she hurried up the street on her high heels. So that a cab driver, stuck at a red light, noticed her and thought of his mother, dead for over twenty years.

Last Campaign

He instructed me to get a copy of his favourite television commercial. Which I did. The one with the twin, teenaged girls selling chewing gum — in their bathing suits beside the pool, enticing identical boys with their double-mint smiles.

I then cut the tape into bite-sized portions, as he suggested, and heaped the bits onto a white dinner plate. Next, I poured Creamy Garlic Salad dressing over the entire lot and fed it to him, one fork full at a time, while standing beside the maroon leather chair across from his Executive desk. I was completely naked. He wore his grey slacks and his new lemon-yellow sports shirt. We were in our sunny office, the front one with a fine view of the parking lot.

The tripod, five feet away, held the Pentax. By a remote controlled cord attached to his foot, he took the colour picture. We were after the Helmut Newton effect: the mannequin-like, naked model, red lips, high heels — the bizarre and dangerous juxtaposition.

Except for the visual distractions of the coffee maker, the filing cabinets and the Trophy fish which hangs behind the desk, the picture turned out quite well. We are planning to feature it on the front cover (full bleed) of our hardware store's Spring Flyer. We believe it will grab market attention in a significant way and stand out from all the other flyers which will soon be circulating through the mail and as newspaper inserts.

Our children and grandchildren are quite supportive of, what just might be, our last advertising campaign. After all, the business is their inheritance and, for the past while, business has not been good. We are, therefore, hoping to revive sales in a dramatic way. Not only that, but we are hoping to avoid staff layoffs. Some of our employees have been with us for over thirty years.

We have told them that we will do whatever is necessary to save their jobs; we appreciate our responsibility and will not whither from it.

Right now, the employees are huddled together in their wretched hopefulness outside the office door. We, in here, are going over the final proofs of the Spring Flyer cover. We think it may have a profound impact on the local community. "Naked Grandmother Sells Pocket Wrenches." The publicity can only help us.

The Early Plastic Shrine

Everything went wrong for the Christmas Party. I got a spot on my liver and had to go to the hospital for tests. By the time they were through with me I was an hour and a half late. Trying to dress was impossible; I couldn't remember how to do it, what went with what. My blue stockings had a tear up the left leg; I put a red top with an orange bottom. Then as I mounted the stairs to my party I had an orgasm on each step. This slowed things up considerably.

Finally I arrived, two hours late for my own party. The Jazz Trio from the Indian Reserve was not doing well, no one could hear them, they were performing away from the crowd, towards the air and the trees. Someone in the crowd yelled out, "They stink!" and then half the guests left. Meanwhile I realised that most of the guests were relatives of in-laws I did not like. Who invited them? I wondered. None of my friends were there. Who invited these semi-strangers and all these eleven-year-old boys eating up the cakes?

My husband said, "We're out of avocados," which meant there could be no more Tex-Mex and I hadn't even started the Chili which was to be served in half an hour's time.

I decided to leave. On my way out I witnessed a conversation between a neighbour on her way in and my mother-in-law standing beside her yellow convertible. "I wouldn't bother with the party," my mother-in-law was saying, "chances are the toilet bowl hasn't even been cleaned."

I visited my friend, the priest. He'd just come off a long shift with a dead man. "I thought that soul would never leave," he said, "it just kept flying around the kitchen like a piece of white blubber, banging into the kitchen cupboards, scaring the budgie."

"We made love on his colonial chesterfield. Outside, snow was falling, one perfect flake at a time.

The priest told me, "Christmas is a good time to die. I can always tell when a soul is ready to leave a dead man, it begins with the eyes. The furrows between the brows become a canyon and the eyes pale and stare almost erotically."

While he kissed me, warts grew on my lips.

I spent the rest of the night at the Early Plastic Shrine of Leo H. Baekland in Yonkers, New York. There, beneath a giant replica of a bobbin end made in 1912 by combining clean phenolic resin with formaldehyde to create the first truly synthetic plastic, I slept.

I dreamed I was a child of the mid-twentieth century, waiting around for science fiction to come true. I was riding in my personal helicopter; the traffic in the heavens was so congested that fleeing souls were crashing into helicopter blades like demented sea gulls. The pillage was awful; priests by the submarine load had to be called in to place wreaths of plastic bananas at the grave sites.

Leo H. Baekland invited me to dinner. We sat down on the roof of his two storey laboratory to carve a turkey dinner the size of a gelatine capsule.

"There is nothing new under the sun," he said, handing me my half of the pill.

"Not true," I screamed. "Don't I have Science Digest? Isn't something new promised every month? And right here beside the ad for fibre optics, doesn't it promise new works, new suns?"

"New things are treacherous," said Leo H. Baekland, "newly invented things, insisting on the future. Possibly we could have done without plastic."

Suddenly I was having a nightmare; it was frightening to think of living on without some wonderful anticipation, some happy surprise, some new gadget.

I stood at the end of a long black tunnel and shouted to my friend, the priest, and to Leo H. Baekland: "Waiting around for science fiction to come true is a lot more satisfying than waiting around for death." I was crying.

Their laughter cut the night like a musical saw. "Booze, dope, technological fixes, it's all the same to us," they said.

The doctor woke me up.

"Here," he said, removing me from the Early Plastic Shrine, "we'll just attach this plastic tubing to your brain and pump you full of someone new to be. It won't take long and I believe you're an isolated case. I don't believe that what you've got is easily transmitted; you'll be back at your party in no time."

childless

they all want to be our child they are lining up on the patio all manner of them wanting to be our child bouquets of red heads small dainty boys the girls are putting on wigs and doing dances the boys are spinning in circles until they faint all day long they call to me play something on the piano and hand me sheet music through the open living room window I am obliging I play something of Beethoven's or a lively Irish jig then they do cart-wheels on our front lawn hoping I'll notice and pick the best one when the telephone rings they rush in clamouring to answer it the lucky one laughing gets to say it's for you Mommy I can't decide I can't decide which one to take they do not have names yet these children my husband will be home soon I have to pick a child before he comes home one child he's out taking pictures of Captains for his scrap book all day long he roams the docks snapping as long as he can find a new Captain to snap he's happy it doesn't matter what kind of boat the Captain is in charge of although he prefers submarines my husband has agreed reluctantly that I can pick one child I've got to decide by suppertime my husband is so particular what if he doesn't like my choice all the children are adorable there's a tiny girl doing somersaults outside my window a tiny girl there's a twelve-year-old boy sitting in a row boat on our front lawn no water just sitting in the boat gazing out upon the wide suburban sea my husband would like him I know he could make the boy Captain of the row boat they could spend many happy hours together snapping perhaps my husband will reconsider and allow me to pick two children one each and I could have the tiny red-wigged girl all day long I could sit at the piano playing *Für Elise* while she dressed in feathers and net could perform cart-wheels handsprings on my living room carpet calling out to me over and over with her sweet tiny voice Mommy Mommy watch me do this I've got to decide by supper time my husband will be home then it's my only chance

bed

who are all these dead people at the foot of my bed? they're shoving one another three old women and a small skinny boy all trying to push one another off my bed the boy is crying shrieking why does no one come? four dead people shouldn't be here they should be on their own beds I'd get up and bite them but I haven't got the strength why won't they leave me alone? they're laughing at me crawling up the bed trying to get my purse I'm scared if I shout they'll grab me push me into the sea the sky overhead is blue I'm sitting in a deck chair beside my mother she's wearing pearls a summer dress smile she's saying you needn't look so glum life's a song there's still time left to sing it overhead a spotlight maybe that's the sun I'm old my eyesight blurs no it's a light switching on switching off don't tell me the dead don't speak my mother's standing at the foot of my bed hold my hand she's saying the journey ahead is smooth and long there are four dead people in a row-boat bobbing in the sea hurry up jump in they're calling why does no one come? I wish the dead were people I knew instead the light keeps switching on switching off my mother's swimming towards the foot of my bed come on come on I can't swim past these pillows I'm crying I haven't got the strength my mother's in the water waving splashing the water feels so warm come on you silly girl jump in the dead are cheering wildly mouths of rust at me mouths of dust it's time it's time it's time

Happy Birthday

I asked my husband to hang from the bedroom window by his feet. Our window is quite high off the ground so there would be a certain amount of hazard involved in this gesture. I wanted a crowd gathering and, being in a hurry, having my husband hang from the window was the quickest way I could think of to achieve this end. I had in mind a silent, reflective crowd, rather subdued, no riotous interplay between the crowd participants, none of that.

I hung my husband from our bedroom window head first, naked. The nakedness, a sure touch, I felt. I wanted a crowd gathered WONDERING: a throng of giant Shasta Daisies, their feathery heads turned upwards, swaying in the morning breeze. A gesture which would impress my neighbours with its originality.

For their part, my neighbours are an ordinary lot; on Mondays they string their husbands out on clotheslines and let them flap in a brisk wind; on Saturdays they paint them daffodil-yellow and plant them singly along the sidewalks of our street — stiff soldiers rat-a-tatting along as far as the eye can see. No crowd gatherings possible with these crude offerings.

As for myself, I will grasp at the inspired gesture wherever I can find it so don't give me a boring bouquet of husbands for my Happy Birthday or two dozen chocolate-covered husbands asleep in a red satin box, either. I wouldn't appreciate it.

instruments of wood and wind

ah, the wind, you say.

blasts of it are stiff against you hair whips your jaw and mouth your sweater tightens and your body jerks in the marionette dance of gusts and lulls you stand off to the left in a clearing at the edge of the cliff.

this high place belongs to you this sea below, a bowl of darting light catches all the blue from your glitter eyes moss swarms at your feet this world is yours. you have travelled always here, stood here an outcrop of beauty and will.

i have seen eagles sway back on the wind at the shout of your laughter

i have seen the tide draw away like a grinning mouth when you lifted your arms.

and i have seen you drink from milky clouds that scudded the clean sky at your bidding and foamed your cheeks with their spume of water and air.

and i have seen trees shrug out of the shadows and stand with you naked, their bark a sudden sheen their/ limbs spinning a parasol over head.

****

the high wind falls your body is loose and trembling. the tremors rise like wavelets like surf and you shimmer another wind starts somewhere i feel it it runs under the sky at you

this javelin wind arcs and hums a single speeding note it hits you the trees are stripped of their bark and their dark blood is slow to surface on such mammoth wounds but you.

you grow thin and flat and hard

you grow deceptive as paper birch and for a moment believe you will outlast the fists and kicks of your beloved wind.

you open the flat of your mouth your tongue rips through the sheet of your face. . .

you fly apart

the wind rolls and throws itself down the receding chins of rock and smashes into the calm sea

i've fallen and lie clenched as a sea star to the green moss. there is nothing in the air no movement no sound no carried smell i open an eye

a new wind hits the stand of pine and a kind of spectacular applause ensues

Charioteer

Jack Stram grew up with heroes. He believed. As a boy he banked his shelves with bubble gum cards. Mantle and Williams and Kaline. All men bigger than life. Bigger than their own insides, Jack would say. He saw some of them play from box seats at Briggs Stadium. Those Saturday afternoons he and his father sailed the Ambassador Bridge in the '59 Plymouth, a pink-finned whimsy soaring into 12th street hardball. Jack watched the men play, effortless figures in performance, bits of white light on gem green.

In damp winter another kind of man deepened Jack's vision. Lindsay and Howe. Strongmen, endurance men using their sticks discreetly, in the corners, to blast a hidden rib. And fly away down the ice to score with a gentle wrist shot. The Olympia. His father parked some distance away and never locked the black Dodge Coupe against the night.

As an adolescent Jack joined in prayer another hero. Inauguration Day. John Kennedy bestowed goodness, gave wonder, christened joy. This new man bonded Jack's heart to his own. Jack believed. Jack loved. Even his father's eyes teared during the American anthem. They were close that year, Jack taking the front seat. They rode strong and low in the grey Imperial. Yankee-bred Canadians.

Then Jack fell beyond love when Kennedy was slaughtered in Dallas. The news cracked over the school PA system. He was in homeroom, history 10th grade, casually viewing the ancient spider-licked film, Julius Caesar. He went home. They all went home. In his living room Jack watched Oswald's face brace against death and for a moment Jack Stram became Jack Ruby. It wasn't until later he knew the profound futility of a small death. He accompanied the caisson through Washington streets a hundred times. On television, radio, in Life. He watched the split-screen stills of murder slamming into the tousled head. For years Jack never wondered why she wore her husband's stain throughout the day, throughout the night, coming north in Texas pink, bringing the body home. That winter his father left Jack alone, dealt the Chrysler away for a stonesilver Polaris.

But Jack Stram recovered his need to believe. With a hungry heart he took up with brother Bobby and Martin Luther King. He marched and sang in his bachelor suite. He bloomed and often he lay wanton in sleep, like a child. He was twenty when they died. The year Dad tooled the country in his needle-nosed Barracuda.

Jack went a long time alone after 1968. He married and fathered two sons. He acquired his career in marketing. But his horror bore inward. The shape of him changed to accommodate great loss. No one to lead.

His father retired with full pension and knocked around town, from golf course to Legion, gassing up the heavy blue Cordoba. Sunday football and roast beef dinners. An occasional game of snooker.

He ran out of things to do. So he bought the boat, a catamaran powered with an 85-horse Johnson. And rammed it, open-throttled, into a concrete dock one drunken summer night.

Jack buried the man under a canopied sky in July. Bearers and mourners wore suits. The Legion men were pressed into uniform. Jack went home.

In the night he dreamed a dream of faces. Of Jesus Christs and Pips and Hardy Boys. Of Mickey Rooney and Pimpernell and Father Casey Muldoon. He dreamed the James Gang and the Three Musketeers. He dreamed the face of time.

In the morning Jack drove his father's car west down Riverside Drive, clipping the miles. Behind the wheel at last.

Hummingbird

She loved it, this baby who flitted from corner to corner against the ceilings of her house. She loved it, surely. She was its mother. She didn't love its mouth dragging down her breasts and cracking open her nipples, the spit-up curdled milk tracking lazily down her shoulders and soaking her shirts, she didn't love the crying or all the diapers, the sweet yellow shit she wiped off with a warm damp cloth. She did love the gurgles of its pleasures, its fat extremities, its bow-legs and the soft spot on its fuzzy warm skull. She loved the idea of ten miniature fingers and toes. But she loved it best when it ascended because it was always happy, always supremely cherubic in air. She was frightened to take it for a walk in the stroller. What if? In the bakery? At the park? Already she had discovered it in the eaves of the attic, hovering beneath the splintery wooden roof. She wished it would take her up, with her suitcase of baby supplies, with her stretch marks and milk-plumped breasts. She kept the placenta in a wooden bowl in the refrigerator. She buried it beside the tomatoes in the garden. The baby dipped and flew curlicues through the leaves of the pear tree above her head. The beat and silvery breeze of its wings swept over her and she stood, lifting her arms. Her hands dripped birth blood and dirt. The baby she surely loved rose and rose, rose and rose.

Seaweed

Swimming down into her body I was another woman altogether, spoiled with rapture. Her shy pink feet were against my back; she was whispering about rain. I was coming to Vancouver like a slow wave. She wore her breasts as a necklace: sliding herself about my head she said I love you, I love you as I love apricots. For a moment it was true. I was a beach and she loved fruit: I turned into a coconut. She broke me open and drank. Everything was wet. Even the air was watery. She was very blond and her eyes were blue. In her ears were seven circles. I opened her mouth, her thighs, her small shell toes. I kissed the palm of her hand; fortunes rose like underwater bubbles and tickled my skin. How I wanted her. I was a dolphin, I was grey with the surge of her tides and had an anthropomorphized snout.

She was my first human being.

Smorgasbord

My mother ate cats. It is a sad truth, one that for many years I could not admit. When she was in a certain kind of mood, watch out cats. She caught them and killed them and ate them raw or she cooked them. She liked them best with Worchestershire and wine sauce. She preferred Siamese cats. Alley cats would do in a pinch but Siamese cats were what she craved. Or manx cats, since she never ate tails anyway. She got her cats from the SPCA. She hoped one of her children would also eat cats but we didn't, even as babies we would rather have starved. Kids are funny that way. We also never did drugs. We just grew up while our mother went on eating cats. Then we had children, perfectly normal children who also did not eat cats. Although, admittedly, my youngest niece was born with ear mites.

Vermilion

My wife painted a fresco in our living room and now my wife needs surgery on her hands. Those two things are not related. Her nerves were not damaged by plaster and pigment work; her problem, the doctor says, is intrinsic, a degenerative disorder that robs her of tactile sense and causes her pain.

My wife's name is Mary. You have probably seen her signature on canvases but if you haven't it doesn't matter. I wish no one did; I wish my wife had never sold a painting, not one painting.

There are words I wish I had never heard, too: chartreuse, I wish I had never heard the word chartreuse. Turquoise is another one. That word turquoise goes right inside me. Vermilion. Is there another word that goes to work on a man like vermilion does?

But I'm a man who appreciates a good kiss, all right. I like a good kiss as well as the next man. What man wouldn't appreciate a kiss? An excellent kiss can make a man overlook words like chartreuse. This is just the way of things. In this world a wife and a kiss and a sunset make a fellow stop. They make a fellow stop in his tracks just outside some doorway and they make his eyelids widen.

Let us say the sunset seen through the window was vermilion.

Let us say my wife Mary was kissing someone else.

Let us say her damaged hands were against the breast of an artist named Diane.

This is the truth.

The truth is two women were kissing and Diane's shirt was undone and her breasts were bare. My wife's hands fit Diane's breasts perfectly; I saw how well they fit. They fit so well an artist could have drawn them as parts of Diane's body.

One of Diane's paintings is of a chartreuse figure poised on the edge of a globe, bending over. My wife Mary's fresco is turquoise.

This is just how it happens, a man turns one corner too many in his life and then it happens, that kiss, and he doesn't know how to act or what to say. He hits his chest with the flat of his hand over and over, he does that.

Here is a photograph: a man, a woman and a woman. Here is a sculpture: a man, a woman and a woman. Here is a story: a man, a woman and a woman. Here is a painting by a woman named Diane. Here I am. Here is my wife, Mary.

In the photograph I age and age. Soon I am fifty. Soon I am eighty-four. Soon I am a hundred and two. I am lucky to be so old, such a very old man with a thin windpipe.

Holy Water

He was a vampire and to open his wife's skin he used either his teeth (he had false incisors) or a razor blade. At night, while the moon pulsed in the sky like a heartbeat, he drank his wife's blood. It was a conjugal thing.

Another vampire, a woman, agreed HIV infection was an occupational hazard, though stomach acids were thought to be reliable in killing the virus. "What can we do?" she cried, lifting her white hands. "We're blood drinkers!"

The first vampire thinned his lips. "We're not," he told the audience, "promiscuous. My wife and I waited 'til our honeymoon. I'm faithful to her. She'd divorce me if I drank another woman's blood."

There was a werewolf on the panel too, but he'd been exorcised.

Haiku House

We live in candlelight, the light of a skinned animal left on the forest floor. At Auschwitz the building in which valuables taken off the dead were stored was known as "Canada." Animals and people stripped of their skins.

My daughter's face looks clean until we get outside (sleepydust in her eyes, streak of milk on her upper lip, bit of dried mucus in her nostril). The darkness is intensified by the bruises on our legs (edges of desk, crib, bed, sofa).

In the middle of the apartment a lamp is on. Here, beside the window, birchbark light. Direct sunlight never enters, but at two in the afternoon the sun strikes the windows of the building opposite and for twenty minutes bounces across into this room. While it lasts it is silvery, metallic, very beautiful. Moonlight, says Alec.

Living in semi-darkness, the accumulation of it, so many inches a year, so many feet.

It's much cooler at this end of the apartment. The window faces north, the floor is an uncarpeted subfloor, the basement directly below. I have my desk here beside the bed. I get up early, turn on the grow light in the kitchen, make coffee and carry it down here to my desk where there are pictures of snow, caribou, Yellowknife in winter and summer.

summer snow: children out of windows.
four in the last twenty-four hours.

haunted by the snowfall in a husky's
delicate eyes. New York. June.

In my bed my daughter surrounds herself with all her possessions — red shoes, purse, two bags — as though her bed is an Inuit grave and she is on a long voyage to the underworld. In Inuit folklore children grew out of the ground as flowers do. "Women out wandering found them sprawling in the grass and took them home and nursed them."

I wear a long summer skirt with a pattern of gray leaves which grow up my legs and into my lap.

The apartment is like a long piece of bamboo — light comes in at either end, but not much — a haiku house — one long seventeen-syllable line.

Baby

We arrive at the hospital around midnight. Now and again I hear the doctor's voice in the hallway. I have a postcard, Still Life with Apple. I focus on the apple, and later the doctor says I'm the most controlled patient she has ever had. Jews are the noisiest she said — she is Jewish — Jews and Italians, and Asian women are the quietest. Canadians, quieter still.

The labour nurse rushes to catch up — a flurry off to the right. She grabs my shoulder and pulls me further upright, whacks my head down against my chest, and yells, Push through your bottom! Push through your bottom!

The patient across from me, seventeen years old and already with a small daughter, is resting to avoid a premature birth. She wages a telephone battle with her family the whole time. At two a.m. she is yelling into the phone, "If you drink all my sodas, I'll kill you. I had twelve sodas when I came in here, and they'd better be there still. Now give me Mommy."

Two a.m. Barred light through windows, shadows on the bed, baby sucking, wind blowing through an empty womb. I adjust a diaper under the other breast to catch the drips. My shoulders are cold. The air — grainy, white, as though the room is an old film, black and white, barely moving.

Strange and interrupted night life. A displaced child nursing a child displaced.

Writing in 1884 about the Central Eskimo, Franz Boas compiles a list of customs. The mother gives birth alone; cuts the umbilical cord alone, either with a stone spear head or by tying it through with deer sinews; eats nothing for five days except meat killed by her husband or by a boy on his first hunting expedition; remains excluded from her own house until a few days after the birth. Loneliness — isolation — all in the context of that snowy light. The sensation, those nights soon after giving birth, that I contained nothing but weather.

Yesterday I spoke slowly as though it was late at night rather than mid-afternoon, the words slow to come, and often wrong. I spoke with Theresa about the trap of motherhood. We wouldn't wish them away yet how changed our lives are. How hard not to be able to do what we want to do. Do people just suspend their lives, Theresa asked, until their children are grown? Appalled at the way her life has already been suspended. Is it terrible to want something more?

Her small face, short dark hair, hands cupped around a mug, sitting only because forced to. She had forgotten her keys and was waiting for David to come home and let her in. Under the conversation ran her counting: the minutes as they went by, the months without daycare, the years without a job. Her eyes, as we drank tea, stayed stirred up by her counting. Measuring her resentment (against David who had said he would be there in an hour and wasn't after two) in that tiny fluorescent kitchen, which isn't even fluorescent yet appears to be.

Winter is coming. Windows, difficult to open, are closed. The leaves of the tree of heaven (scrawny city sumac) turn yellow. I switch out the kitchen light and walk to the front of the apartment, to this pale light, too pale for October, November light in October (we've missed another season).

The Inuit word for starvation means in between. In between summer and winter when it was hard to hunt — the snow too soft, ice too treacherous. In between lives — this period with a new life which isn't my own.

Precipitation

The baby often stretches his hand towards the window that overlooks the street. When I take him over there, holding him so that he can see out, he smiles and croons to the window and me.

Wet snow. Flakes as big as cigarette papers on the corner of 105th and Broadway. We stand under umbrellas, and I remember David Thompson's comment that melting snow is wetter than rain; it penetrates a tent in a way that rain never does.

Beautiful — this precipitation that is more than rain and less than snow.

Light is falling, I say to Sochi. I look out the window as she sits up in bed. She peers out too — at the slice of pale light which touches the gray brick wall five feet beyond her window. Light falls like rain — an outside condition which never enters. We measure the inches.

Nature Scenes

Silence follows the loud click of the trap. We lift our heads and listen, absolved of further action.

Alec disposes of the mouse. And now I hear more noises in the kitchen cupboard, and brace myself for another trap, and further possibilities.

A friend got a phone call at five in the morning. Her neighbour sobbed into the phone, "Maria! There's something in my ear. I feel it moving!" Maria got up and drove her to the emergency room. On the way there, and while they waited two hours to see a doctor, Maria's friend pressed her hand against her ear, and rocked back and forth, and cried. When the doctor looked in her ear, his expression didn't change and he didn't say a word. He went off, came back with a pair of tweezers, reached into her ear, and pulled out a cockroach, "THIS BIG!" said Maria. Then he pranced around the room yelling, "The first woman to give birth to a cockroach! The first woman to give birth to a cockroach!"

Ever since, the neighbour has slept with cotton in her ears. Alec said, What about her nostrils?

Pigeons nest on the sills of the bricked-over windows of the building beside us. A building crew has begun to bash open the windows. They work from the inside and use mallets. I watch one window buckle and give way; they start on another. A single pigeon, still too young to fly, sits on the sill. With each blow the baby jumps. Its mother swoops down, the baby cranes up in ecstasy, she gives it food and flies off.

We watch this scene from the kitchen window, one domestic grouping watching another domestic grouping. I think to myself, There are too many pigeons in New York, and look away. After a while I say, Maybe we should tell them. Alec shrugs, They won't be able to do anything. A few minutes late I say, We should tell them. Alec sticks his head out the window and yells, "There's a baby pigeon on the window sill." The worker yells back, "There's nothing I can do about it." And our daughter asks, "What did he said?"

The Met

Steam rises off the fountain at Lincoln Center, a Christmas tree blazes with illuminated musical instruments, a young man makes cappuccinos across the street. The young man is slender, rather short, olive-skinned, with an open shirt and a lovely display of chest hair. He heats the milk in a metal container, pours it into a tall slender white cup, adds the espresso, then the cinnamon.

I sit at the counter and watch him. The open shirt has light and dark gray stripes on a white background. He makes two other cappuccinos while I drink mine. To my right rich chocolate cakes are displayed in a glass case. I pull out a scrap of paper from my pocket and jot down: memory of baking two Black Forest cakes in Yellowknife — midnight, one a.m., two a.m., the layers came out of the oven. My birthday. 25.

A homeless woman comes in. She says something to the waiter behind the counter, then waits. After a few minutes she goes to the man at the cash register. Are you the manager? He nods. She says, I asked to see the manager and the waitress told me to wait and went off. I'm listening, he says. More quietly she asks, Do you have any coffee, food? The manager speaks to the cappuccino maker. Give her what she wants, he says. The cappuccino maker puts a cup of coffee in front of her, and she recoils: "Not that!" The manager looks up. To go, he says.

Eros

He climbs out of the sea carrying nothing more than a handful of sand. He looks old and tired as if he has swum a long way. There are bruises on his body, small sad ones that are no larger than a dime. Naked, he stands with his toes buried in sand. There is no boat behind him no one calling him back or ahead. The sun makes him shield his eyes with his hand. In the distance he can see a rider approaching on a horse. He stands there counting the strides of the horse. Does he expect news or injury? It is hard to tell because nothing on his face reveals what he is thinking. His body calculates a few simple arithmetic operations and he slowly falls to his knees. Soon the horse and rider have found an exit on the horizon and he kneels there with hand still full of sand and the one clue that he has come this far for something.

Once he was the lover of a woman with red eyes. Once he could swim the sea in a single stroke. Once he could set fire to the world with a single breath. Once he was the first existing without childbirth emerging from the sea standing sad and alone on the shore watching the moon draw lines on the shore. He lifted up a handful of sand and found his name there. He is old now abandoned unsure of what he set in motion. Somewhere up the beach a hotel waits with five empty rooms and in one a young woman sits before the mirror behind her a child waiting as her mother combs her hair. In her hand she has a small doll. Once in awhile the child fiddles with her hair or looks out the window at the sea. Down on the beach a small figure waits kneeling in the sand as if before an altar. The child loses interest and looks back at her mother a few sparks now and then singing out in her hair. The child goes to the mother's side and smiles at her. The mother is still unsure of how she can leave her daughter here. She thinks of the old man at the shore and speaks to him in her mind. "Go, it is too late she does not want to know her father. She is safe here and dry. Your wet hands would only frighten her. GO now. She is learning to play and that is important. All you can do is frighten her." As if he has heard her the man backs into the water slowly looking straight into the hills as if he knew exactly where the sun would be in the morning. Slowly he sinks again into the water knowing it is someone else's turn to find out. The child knows her father only as a separation. He is a voice her mother has described to her at night before bed. In her dreams he stands tall before her without words or disguises. A beard reaches down to his chest. In his hand he holds the world and points to it saying "Inside here is everyone's dream even this one. Don't let them out or speak to anyone of this. I will be back later to see what you have done with this. For now remember I am always overhead." With that he turned into her mother waking her in a hotel not too unlike this one near the sea. The waves outside sounding like the earth's heartbeat.

Apollo

On his deathbed, he remembered being a teenager and what it was like to have a god for a father, someone who could change your thoughts while you slept. There had been ideas he'd had as a teenager, ideas that now seemed silly but then they were powerful and new, coming from a part of himself his father didn't know. They were wild ideas. His father wasn't a bad father, just didn't know how to deal with a son who had ideas of his own. One night he was visited by the Muses and they left magical notes on his lips. In the morning when he spoke it was in musical notes. His father went to his side and kissed his hands as if he knew that his son was saved at last. But the son ran out of the house into the street as if he were pursued by an angel of fire. The boy never sang to his father or ever allowed him to come near him again. Yet everywhere he went, the music followed him and made him feel a captive of his own gift. Now near death he can feel the music finally leave him and he wishes his father was here so that he could speak to him and kiss him. Turning away from life and toward death like a sleeper turns from one side to the other, he sees his father standing in the distance with outstretched hands singing in his soft voice all his son's notes. In death, the old man knew that there has to be a time when we step back and know that only our parents know the world before we came to it.

Ares

My father died before I was born. His last breath expired in the same bed where I was born. My mother was my father all of my life. She would show me how he walked and talked and I could only see her there. She had such tender small eyes but when she played my father she stretched them so they looked hard and precise. Her mouth when it wore his words was cruel and large. She loved my father until she died. She said his name with her last breaths. By then her hands were frail and yet she lifted one to my shoulder and smiled as if my father were standing just behind me.

She never had a picture of him except what she carried in her mind. But she never wavered in her vision of him. I don't know if I would have loved my father or even liked him. I am not my mother and can't say that I love men the same way she did. Sometimes my father speaks to me but it is always with my mother's voice. He never says anything about love though, just about how he misses the shine in my eyes although he has never seen them. I have a son of my own now and he walks in a way I know my father would have. I'm not sure if I like that although I have never tried to do anything about it. I know my father was rough and callous even though my mother never told me that. I could tell by the way she changed when she talked about him. It was the roughness that took his life. When my son is rough I tell him to be gentle but he soon forgets and is rough again with the cat or one of his friends. But he is never rough to me just holds me so tight at night before he goes to bed.

I never visit my father's grave although I visit my mother's often. When I am there with my son he says: "Grandma can you hear me? Grandma can I visit you for awhile. I've never been in heaven before." Later he asks me if grandma can hear him and I answer yes even though I am not sure myself. At night when my son is asleep I sit and think about the lessons that mothers and fathers pass on. And sometimes I wish that my father had lived so I would know for sure the power he had in his hands. But I only know what my mother has shown me and that is not how one should find one's father. Even if he was cruel, I would like to know that for sure since I find it hard to trust what is cruel inside me. Perhaps from him I could have learned that there is something to do with it.

Out of Time

I get shot out of a cannon for a living. Tonight Alice comes to my room before the show. It is the first time I have seen her since the divorce. She asks if I would mind if she took Leslie for the whole summer. Alice plays with her hair and for a long time I don't say anything just look at her through the mirror as if practising where to look when I turn around. Finally she picks up a picture of the two of us together. I'm not sure why I leave it around perhaps to frighten myself or to stop the room from changing. She laughs and asks, "Did I really look like that then?" In the picture she looks as if she were hiding from the camera ashamed of something. We never really lived together merely shared a few rooms, bought a few pieces of furniture. Some nights we would stay up all night repairing what others had done to us. After making love we would both keep our eyes tightly closed until morning.

When Alice moved out I knew that Leslie would stay with me even though my job was dangerous and she was not my paternal child. Alice liked to change things suddenly: "Wipe the slate clean" she was fond of saying. By that time Leslie was already in grade 3 and I was comfortable with everything even the danger every night and the travelling. Leslie would watch me practise plugging her ears and smiling at the same time and the only thing I was afraid of was that I might disappoint her or that some night I might land and not see her smiling, her head turned into the crowd not wanting to see her father broken into pieces. She doesn't come to the shows anymore. She's stopped being frightened by what I do, tells her friends that I work in a factory that makes sausages. Some nights I hear her crying but I'm too afraid to ask her why.

Alice is still playing with her hair and looking at the picture. I turn around and I know I have no choice and I say, "Fine Alice if that's what you want" and I could pound my fist, but all I do is listen as Alice turns to me quietly the nylon of her pants rubbing as she turns. She doesn't smile or say a word just puts the picture down and bends over to kiss my forehead and as I look up at her I wonder why it takes us so long to learn that we are always alone. She moves towards Leslie's room and I hear again the tweaking of her pants as she walks. I wish for a moment I had kissed her hard on the mouth and sucked her breath in with mine tasted what I fear the most.

Catching the News

The house is knee-deep in papers and clippings. They rustle when you walk. Daily they fall and settle in layers over the floor, over tables and chairs, desks, beds. The lawn outside is littered. You think it best to try to work anyway, forget the distractions. A thud on the step outside. A train crash lands in the space cleared by the opening and closing of the front door. *Rush Hour Horror*. Right there on your door mat. Bringing the world to you. You can hear the sirens as you pick it up. You take it inside. To tell the truth you are always one or two disasters behind. Lockerbie, Zeebrugge, Uttar Pradesh, Kutayah. Names that mean nothing until The Journal has spoken to the survivors.

Still you like to make an effort. Though you do wonder. A plane falls from the sky on an autobahn, jamming the highway, the airwaves, jamming the eyelids open. Minoltas and Nikons explode at the crash site. And in Los Angeles the driver of a vehicle on the freeway, seeing a young woman out of gas, reverses to assault her in the privacy afforded by a hedge. *Thousands believed dead in chemical explosion in India*. But in Toronto Mrs. Patel is having her nostrils cut with dressmaking scissors while the men who broke in look for something to steal. And in Montreal. In Montreal.

You put the plane crash on top of the raft of loose papers where the hall table might be, covering a picture of children who sleep in cardboard boxes. Who could do with the insulation. Newsprint, newsprint. You shuffle a way through to the kitchen — you cleared it yesterday but you can't win. Sunday will roll around with a new slab of horror. This one specially formulated for the hash brown set. Family fare from Great Britain. *Ninety-three dead in football terror*. The terraces tumbling like dominoes, the stands folding like fans. A pair of arms waving up from the ground like the stalks of lilies. Talk of nothing else down at the pub while the Yorkshires rise in the beef dripping. You still haven't found the kettle. *The body of a five-year-old boy who is believed to have suffocated in the mud as his attacker* — the kitchen is such a mess.

You find the kettle and put it on for coffee. You can't work without coffee. Keeps the heart palpitating. *Four-day-old calves fed diet of chocolate-flavoured pig's blood*. The things you read. You can't stomach breakfast. Can't think for thinking. The state of our slaughter-houses. Can't write. Not even a protest letter. *Arms sales up*. There's so much paper in this house it's a hazard. You've tried keeping it to one room but it travels. Someone always forgets and opens the door. It drifts out. When it gets deep it's easy to miss things, fall down a step, slip into a crevass. Who would know?

The coffee spills on an oil spill. Special effects. Bigger than Valdez. You begin to riffle, rummage. There's a story here somewhere. Story of a lifetime. If you could find it. *Wall falls on family of four.* So much to read before you get to it. You never finish anything. The opening paragraph is always enough. It always leads to the same place. All you can say is "God." It isn't any help. You don't talk to each other any more, don't make love. You spread the papers out in front of you, between you, lick your (own) middle fingers and start turning. Jeez. Shaking your heads. Sometimes you trade. You always come out even. God.

He's All Right But His Wife

Yes you'd be surprised. Not quite you know. But then she had Art so that explains it. Yes a few years ago. Didn't you know? No you can't tell by looking. If she's brushed her hair. She covers it up well. Had it quite badly apparently. They thought she was painting at first but it turned out she was writing. Took them quite a while. She used to go off by herself. Whole days. It could have been fatal of course. She was lucky they stopped it in time. He was wonderful. Gave her a few quick babies. They chewed up all the blank paper and swallowed the pencil stubs. It *seemed* to work all right. Of course you can never tell with something like Art. It tends to come back doesn't it. Can break out anywhere once it's started they say. Anytime. Terrible thing. I mean for all we know she's still got it. Just a trace I mean. And still some of the symptoms I think. They're supposed to persist too. You know, word after word after word

Finding the Body

She thought how lucky they were never to have found one. Everyone else had. She thought that twenty years or more had somehow proofed the house. It was not exciting living in a proofed house. Better, though, than the sudden shock, tripping one night over it in the dark on the way to bed with a glass of cold water. What she hadn't bargained for were the leaks, the cracks that came along with twenty years. Because somehow the thing had got in, seeped in it must have over time, slowly to reassemble itself there on the living room floor. There had been nothing to see at first, nothing to detect but an ill-defined staleness. She had to open doors. Then it seemed there was something there, some kind of obstruction, a gathering, a darkening right there in the middle of the floor. It meant a detour on the way to the bathroom, a little skirting chassé so as not to stumble. The children didn't notice a thing. Ran right over it. Through it? The trampling feet. It was immaterial. She asked him leading questions — do you think the carpet could do with cleaning? shall we move the sofa? — to see if he had seen it too. He said probably. Then one day when the sun came out she saw it quite plainly. There's a corpse in the middle of the living room, she said. He said I know. I was thinking of moving out. She considered for a moment lying down beside the corpse, to make two. I think we should try to revive it she said. The kiss of life. Too late, he said, not relishing the lips, or a tussle with stiff limbs. Then let us get it out of the house, she replied. And so together they bent and lifted the thing, which was lighter than it looked but slipped about inside its suit, making it difficult to handle. And its limbs, as he had feared, were stiff and most awkward to manipulate, and its head lolled, which was most pathetic, and the smell of it made her nose burn and her eyes water until, as they reached the back steps which were wet with rain, she thought they might all three slip and fall among the dustbins. I can't do this, she said, overcome suddenly as she had not been in years with a tidal wave of love for all things, but especially the two of them, which were living, and therefore dying.

The We-Must-Be-Crazy Birthday Sale!

Price Crash on Entire Range of Mid-Life Crises!!

I want one
   I want one of those
      I want one of those on the top shelf

A big one
   Everyone in the street has one
      Everyone's had one for ages
         Debbie had a big one and her husband took her to Florida
I want one I want one I want one get the boxes down
Oh goody
See that one? That one's rad. You just get up one morning, start making the toast and then you put your mouth like this, see? With your teeth together. You pick up the toaster and yank the plug out so hard the tiles fly off the wall then you throw it in the sink. Or there's this one nearly the same only when you start you pick up the laundry and push it down the toilet. There's lots. There's some real heavy duty ones. Like in some you can walk straight out and get on a bus and go DOWNTOWN. It comes with high heels and you get to do all kinds of stuff in the back of people's cars. But Mo had that one and she said it was more boring than going to yoga. This one's better. I want this one. You get to drop the kids off at school and get on a train. Then you go backwards and forwards across Saskatchewan by rail. For two years. Loads of people get on and off and some of them are doing it too and they all talk in their sleep and you get to listen. Yeah, I know you have to like the breakfasts. Open it up.

Waiting For Margot

6:15. Platform thirteen appears and disappears in a choppy sea of bodies. Wait for the wave to recede as the train empties. A space clears. A woman is bending to fix her shoe, a high shiny slingback. She straightens up and it is not you, Margot. For which I am relieved. Else how to pick a way through Truth and Beauty with one of us in four-inch heels, after all these years and carrying all we know, and don't. The right gear essential for a grapple with Life, or Art. No distractions.

She totters away, the woman with the slipping shoe. Off to the heel bar for a quick fix. I stand by the gate to platform thirteen, not sure if I'd know you, you me. Are we older women now? From here see all the faces peering back at me, up over my head to the departures. All the waiting, gazing hopeful.

So crowded now we could miss each other. The tide racing. Must dash. Got to fly. But some still managing to meet others in this surge of loners. Robert! Ja-anice! Getting to grips with each other's shoulder pads, cheeks laid on cheeks. Butterflies. I haven't felt this way in years. There hasn't been time, giving birth, cleaning up. Only surface occasionally, moments like this, drag my self up from under, where it spends its time floundering about on the family shingles. Let it gasp a bit at the bright lights, all the independent, jolly little craft bobbing on the surface. Sorry I can't stay longer. Busy day tomorrow. When what I mean is can't stand all this noise and glitter. Tell me it's the same for you. That you prefer to lie in bed searching with closed eyes for the perfect story while the children downstairs scramble for the last crust, check each other's heads for nits.

Footsteps determined and purposeful behind me. I turn a bright face. Oh, she is so collected and in command. Look at the clothes pressed sharp, oh the clicking heels. She looks right by me, not up at the screen. She knows which train is hers, what's what, who's who, when to say when. You're not like that, are you, Margot? Successful, I mean, coping. For what shall we talk about? Whole tracts of Art will be sealed off We shall have to broach trade figures, the deficit.

A few letters launched across the years would have been a help. In the circumstances. Or perhaps yours did not permit. A brood of children too many to count, or men, strange substances, good causes, debt, untiring devotion, rare disease. Or common. Statistics favour the last. One in three now. Soon be one in two. You or me, Margot.

The display is still humming, flickering over my head, the star-gazers still gazing. You could have sneaked a look, I suppose, while I wasn't watching. Seen me here off guard, a frank moment in a dusty mirror. Decided against it in that split second. So that you had to take a deep breath, plunge back into the crowd and strike out again, head down, for the far shore. I wouldn't blame you. Really.

Life

Monopoly

Clare has only ever wanted the greens and yellows. Her brother and sister try to buy them up first, knowing she's capable of reckless trades to possess them. Boardwalk and Park Place for Marvin Gardens. All the railroads.

Tim likes the utilities.

Janis goes to jail a lot.

The game is as old as their childhood and has suffered as much from it as they have. Canadian Tire money serves as an alternate for much of the Monopoly money. There are pennies and marbles for houses and hotels. The *second prize at the beauty contest* card has teethmarks all through it from the long dead family dog Salome.

Clue

Professor Plum has been replaced with a wine bottle cork and is now called Mr. Pinot Noir. They fight over the cork. No one ever wants to be Mr. Green or Mrs. White. The losers of Mr. Pinot Noir fight over Miss Scarlet.

Janis can't see the point of the candlestick. There's already a lead pipe and a wrench, why have another smashing-in-the-head implement? Why not a blowgun or a car or a small explosive device? Why not a poisoned cocktail?

The Business Game

This is hardly ever played because it's too complicated to understand. The best thing about it is the plastic judge's gavel that has a black and a white marble inside it. To decide the outcome of a business takeover the gavel is shaken by the player attempting the takeover and one of the marbles drops down the shaft of the gavel to the viewing hole at the bottom of the handle.

White for yes.

Black for no.

The gavel is now held together haphazardly with masking tape. Once, Clare and Tim, arguing over the colour of the dropped marble wrestled the gavel to pieces. Even now when they play, Tim, who is thirty-three, will put a hand on his older sister's arm and say "Honestly, it *was* white." Clare will give the same reply she's given for twenty years.

"Liar."

The Dictionary Game

The word is phillumenist.
Clare's definition: "Someone who pastes stamps into an album while in a deep hypnotic trance."
Tim's definition: "A botanist who studies a particular species of small shrub found on the Baltic coast in February."
Janis's definition: "A drainage ditch in ancient Greece."
Tim and Janis pick Clare's definition.
Clare picks Tim's.
No one picks the ancient drainage ditch or "collector of matchbox labels," which is the real meaning of the word.

Life

"Shit," says Clare. "I don't want to be a lawyer. Can't I go again?"
"A lawyer's good," says Janis. "Six. Give me another of those blue pegs."
"Boys," corrects Tim.
"I need an extra car. There's too many of them."
Tim hands over an empty yellow plastic car.
"They're good equity."
"O shit," says Clare. "I just hate being a lawyer when I really am one."
She launches herself at the spinner with such ferocity that her elbow sideswipes one of Janis's cars full of offspring.
"I don't want to go to millionaire acres again. All I want to do is squander and plunder. Pillage. Pillage. Pillage.
What did I get?"

Flash-point

"This had better be good," warns Emma. "There is stuff tonight. That I'm missing."

"A million bulbs," says Mona from the front seat. "Think of it. One million."

"That's more than ten," says Wade. He starts counting, his voice muffled from under the blanket. "One-two-three..." He swings his small legs in rhythm with the numbers. "Four-five-six..."

"Asshole," says Emma.

"Watch your mouth." Mona lurches the station wagon towards the curb.

"He kicked me."

There is a long blast of a car horn.

Mona rolls her window down.

"Asshole," she bellows.

"Ten," says Wade triumphantly.

Mona shuts off the engine and squints at the tape deck.

"What time is it?"

Emma cranes her neck around the headrest.

"8:58."

"Good. Almost 8:00."

"Why don't you fix it? The hour went back ages ago." Emma flops back in her seat.

"Mum, I'm freezing."

Mona rolls her window back up.

"Two minutes," she says. "Two minutes and the Parsons will switch on one million Christmas lights." She bangs a palm against the steering wheel. "Shine up the whole sky."

"I can't see anything," says Wade.

"Take the stupid blanket off your face then." Emma grabs at a corner but Wade just clutches it around himself tighter.

"No!"

"Shut up," says Mona.

There is a sudden flash; so big it kicks a hole right through the smooth bottomed darkness. A flash, and then sharp, quick bursts of sound. And then total blackness. Every house and streetlight, up and down the road, dark. Out.

Mona sits completely still. One million lights. She can't imagine what that would have looked like. She wanted to see. One million lights. Of course it's too much. They must have blown the transformer. Of course. Of course. Of course. She feels as though she is tugging her breath out of her.

Like it is knotted and she can't pull it up through her throat. She is alone and stopped and she can't remember ever not being disappointed. Ever. She feels like crying. She clicks open the door handle. She gets out of the car.

Wade is humming numbers to himself and leaning up against Emma, hoping she won't notice he isn't on his side of the back seat. She smells nice. She's warm and big and her blue puffy coat feels like a pillow. Suddenly the darkness inside Wade's blanket goes hard and white and he feels Emma stiffen beside him. The numbers go out of his head. Gone. He tries to say something but there's nothing slow enough to catch and hold onto.

Emma sees the world go floodlit and hears the gunfire and thinks, 'it's all over.' Wade's crying. Her mother is getting out of the car. Emma just watches. There's darkness so thick outside it seems it could be scooped up and held in open hands.

The Virgins

I mistake the Virgin Mary for a photographer. She's dressed in purple and holds something up to her right eye. It turns out to be a rock, not a camera.

"What's the Virgin Mary doing with a rock?" I ask, but you've already slid into the pew.

There are Virgin Mary statues all around the interior of the church. All colours. Life size, the bodies are obviously from the same mold but the arms are in different positions. The orange Virgin reads a book. The blue Virgin holds a wineglass. I can't really see what the yellow Virgin is doing as she's partially obscured by the pipe organ. It appears that she's folding a towel.

"Back from the laundry," I say, but you don't know what I'm talking about and tell me to shut up.

We're on the groom's side. The bride has a much bigger team. I start counting to see how many we're outnumbered by but lose track at sixty-seven when I spot the green Virgin carrying a pot roast.

"Christ!" I say, and you say "What?" and the music starts. The bride walks slowly down through the gauntlet of plaster Virgin Marys to the altar. The groom is somehow already there. We missed his arrival. The priest opens a blue three-ring binder. Someone off to the left of the priest is slotting big plastic numbers into a wooden display stand. The plastic numbers are the same ones gas stations use to show the price of unleaded. The priest is saying that love is like a bicycle out of control on a steep hill.

"What does that mean?" I hiss. You start to giggle and I have to step on your foot to make you stop.

Then it's suddenly all over. The bride's side is up on their feet, smiling and shaking hands. We attempt this, but since there's only fourteen of us, sparsely planted across one side of the church, it's fairly futile. We stand up, feeling stupid. The bride's team promptly sits down. We sit down. The bride's team leaps to their feet. Several of our team valiantly stand up again. The rest of us glance in confusion at one another, looking for someone who knows the rules. No one seems to.

"When did the married part happen?" you ask, but I have no idea. Somehow we missed witnessing everything we were invited to witness. The bride's side are back in their seats again. Overtop of their heads I can see the red Virgin Mary. Her right arm is extended in front of her body, the palm of her hand tilted up. Cradled protectively in the crook of her left arm is a red football.

Timed Writing

Gross Words
Less Errors
Net Words

     The Prairies are composed of three different and distinct areas of farming. Crops grown and types of farms present are a factor of the quality of the land itself. The bottom corners of Saskatchewan and Alberta are the driest. Dear Karen I'm so bored I can't believe it. I don't think you should still hate me because it isn't fair. I just said that stuff and it doesn't mean it's real. Vast, treeless plains with sandy soil low in organic matter and bunches of short grass covering the top layer of soil. Evaporation is not a factor. I saw Tom S. in the smoking area after gym and I'm sure he still likes you. He was wearing those great faded jeans that make his bum so cute. Water is essential for the survival of all life, human and otherwise. British Columbia is the province which abounds in this natural resource. There are numerous streams, rivers, lakes and marshes. He says that a bunch of them are going cruising Friday night in Chris's van. Maybe he'll ask you. Why else would he tell me? He knows I see you all the time. I'm still your best friend because I didn't mean to call you a bitch. There are hundreds of snowfields, and of course, glaciers, which help to store water for small periods of time. Precipitation in the form of rain and snow also adds to British Columbia's abundant water resources. It's not like it's you or anything that makes me mad. I just get a feeling and it's not your fault but you didn't have to go to the concert with Sandy when you said you'd go with me and No matter where you travail No matter where you travel in the province of Quebec there are the long silver fingers of church spires pointing up into the pale blue sky I didn't say I'd positively go but you could have tried to ask again if you cared but I guess you don't There are other stone structures visible in the province, often some of the finer homes and buildings within a village. I don't see what the big deal is really. It's not the end of the world. Town halls are often especially fine examples of architectural technique and

Riding

5:30 a.m. We have five layers of clothing on and we're frozen. When we left the motel there was frost on the motorcycle seats. Now, half an hour later, our breath has turned to ice on the inside of our helmet visors. We lurch the bikes to a stop, slide our lumpy, padded bodies to the ground and move them in awkward slow motion across the parking lot to the truck stop door.

7:30 a.m. We've been riding lying down, bodies slung over the gas tank, feet jammed up onto the rear passenger pegs. My right hand is clenched in a death grip around the throttle. I hold my left hand against the engine casing, trying to transfer some heat to my stiffened fingers. You have just ridden up beside me, pointing and sounding your horn. We pull into a gas station. My scarf has somehow worked loose and is flapping dangerously close to the bike's rear wheel. I tuck it back in and try to make a reference to Isadore Duncan but my face is numb and the words won't squeeze out between my locked teeth. We push the bikes over to the pumps and fill up with gas.

10:00 a.m. We've stopped for coffee at a service station on the outskirts of Sudbury. We stand out by the bikes. The sun is getting stronger. The cold October air is slowly stirring tepid where it touches our flesh — faces, fingers clamped around the warm styrofoam cups. In the distance is a single smokestack, a sharp exclamation mark in the blank, wide sky.

2:00 p.m. In the diner where we stop for lunch a radio plays songs about Jesus and hearts that are broken. We're still dazed from the noise of wind in our helmets, say 'what? what?' to each other across the table with the sticky plastic placemats that show the cocktails of the world. There are hunters in the restaurant. We parked the bikes next to a box trailer containing a dead bear. A young black bear, spread-eagled in the trailer, each of its four paws lashed with yellow rope to a corner of the box. When the wind gusted across the parking lot it lingered in the fur, lifting it into ridges, whispering the edges, swaying it fluid as though it were a field of soft grass.

3:30 p.m. The bikes lean placidly on their stands either side of me. It's started to rain. We're pulled off onto the side of the highway, frantically rummaging around in saddlebags for our rain gear. The world has darkened alarmingly quickly. All the cars swishing past us have their headlights and wipers on. We stuff ourselves into the plastic pants and jackets, as clumsy as young children struggling into snowsuits.

5:30 p.m.   Ten miles from home and the storm is over. We've just put gas in the bikes and I'm walking back from the cashier's booth to where you wait by the curb. I've peeled the sodden gloves from my hands, which for a week afterwards will be stained black from the leather dye. You're removing your helmet. The bikes glisten in the slow, returning sun. We rode down through the hills north of the city. The sky bubbled, turned green; lightning pinned the open fields. We rode down through the hills; the bikes funnelling the water, parachutes of rain opening behind us.

Painted Day

> "A simile of sky hung like a light blue canvas
> securing the world from outside eyes. The air
> vibrated with the strophes of Spanish guitar music."
> — fragment from an unidentified diary —

Yellow sun painted the white stucco homes, and the red-earth weeping tile on the rooftops shed the remaining drops of a morning sun-shower onto the red cobble-stone road. Morning invaded the corners of the buildings jettisoning residues of night. It was a Picasso day. Perhaps it was a Hemingway day. Not a "Sun Also Rises Day." Not a "blue period" day. But there was no doubt that it was a cubist day — multi-faceted — the kind of day that Gabriel Garcia disregards for it is all too common with no distinguishing features. It was the kind of day that repeats itself in small ways as with the echoes of heels moving to and fro outside the window on the wet, red cobblestones below. The kind of day that one might spend at Gertrude Stein's while Ernest hangs back in the corner watching, lynx-like, fragments of sentences re-arranging his thoughts. The guitar drifts into the room from the plaza below, past the wrought iron window bars, past the gently billowing tied curtains, past the hairs in Gertrude's ears as she passes the tea and talks of minimalist opera and the thingness of things. It was that kind of day, and I was waiting for a phone call. I was waiting for her to call. She was going to call about going for a bicycle ride, we were going to cycle along the Humber river past the insect reeds, the Canada geese, and fading October grass, through the mist-shrouded trees, into the wine-chilled, late-afternoon fall. The sky was a soft blue-grey canvas suspended by irregularly-placed staples. In places, bulges seemed to hang right to the ground. It was a fall day, a "Barometer Rising" day. A day when the senses are as alive to themselves and their own wanderings as they are to the day as it is.

In a movie the night before, an African bushman watching "people-things" through a telescope looked up inquisitively at his microbiologist friend and asked how all those tiny people got inside that small scope. A clean mind before the painting starts, is still a canvas mind, prone to canvas thoughts. It was that kind of day, waiting for the phone to ring. Guitar music drifting past my ears on a Spanish-African day along the protozoan banks of the insect-traced river. I was waiting for a call, my mind already bicycling past the rushing river bank, past plodding painted turtles, shrill red-winged blackbirds through the yellow-mist afternoon. It was a flamenco day.

Getting Weighed

At the grocer's, I walk in to get my usual cup of coffee. The owner says "Hi!" the way he always does. He is talking to a woman who is neatly dressed but in clothes that speak of a quiet poverty. Brown cloth coat, rubber boots, a colourful shawl over the head, babushka-style. The rubber boots to keep the feet dry, if not entirely warm, in the snow and slush. She is doing most of the talking, her round face and plump round mouth popping out words as if they were watermelon seeds. She has a French accent and a gap where a tooth is missing and the words have a swishing sound. I notice that she is gabbing precisely at the spot in front of the coffee counter where I usually go to get my coffee. She gabs about her stay in Paris. She was there for eleven years. "Ahh, the men, and there were always drinks. It was beyooteefull," she says, stretching out the word in front of her like a kid with a piece of bubble gum. "It could've been better financially speaking," she says, "after all, there was the war, but other than that it was..." and she says it again, "beeyooteefull." I am getting a little perturbed. She is in front of me and seems oblivious to my presence. All I want is to get a coffee and get out. I've got work to do. Can't be hanging around listening to some old doll rhapsodising about her past. The owner gestures to her with his eyes, and she says, "Oh, sorry dahlink. I hope I wasn't in your way."

I told her no, and as I reached for the coffee pot I noticed that it was all gone except for a slop of dregs. I also noticed, that as the babushka spoke, she was waving a styrofoam coffee cup with what must've been the last of the coffee. What should've been *my* coffee. The cup bounced in her left hand while she gesticulated with her right. I watched as she spilled coffee onto the counter. The owner noticed that I wanted a coffee, and came around the counter. In a way I was pleased because I'm a bit too used to coffee that's been sitting on heaters for half a day, and he took some beans and ground them and then put the grounds in a fresh paper filter and even though it meant that I'd have to wait for a bit, at least I'd have a fresh coffee. After he poured the water into the machine I tuned in to what the woman was saying. It had something to do with scales. Not lizard scales but the kind that you weigh things on. The kind you have in grocery stores. "Tell me one thing," she said, "how come allatime, they gotta weigh things on scales? What is it with the scales? An apple is an apple. You charge for the apple. A banana is a banana." As far as I could tell she felt that all fruits and vegetables should have the same price. One carrot was as good as another in her mind. And if the customer was smart enough or quick enough to pick out a slightly larger one, then more power to them. At least the quick ones could get a deal. But there was no beating the scales. She said, "They're skinning us with those scales. We haven't gotta chance. Skinning us, like an apple or an orange. Till we're naked!" The owner looked at me poker-faced, apologetic, and rolled his eyes lizard-wise toward the ceiling. And, again, she screamed "Naked!" but in a continental sort of way which, although it was a bit loud, did not seem shocking in any way, rather she seemed to have a well-balanced mixture of indignation and information, and it seemed to me that she had arrived at this point of view on her own. It seemed entirely original to me. I began to notice that she had a kind of understated sophistication. She was worldly. But poor. "Can I have this coffee for free?" she said. And he said, "Yeah, sure, sure, have a coffee, it's on me." He was a good-hearted kind of guy, and I got the sense that he was actually half-interested in what she had to say. It was usually pretty quiet in the store, and he was a talkative sort, helped him pass the time, day in, day out. She had colour in her brown coat and old country shawl. I got the impression that he was only rolling his eyes and acting put-out to humour me and not because he was intolerant of her, even if she was a bit eccentric. "Taking off our skins, that's what they're doing!" she said. "They weigh *us* too!" She screamed. By now the coffee had filled enough of the pot for me to fill up my cup. "Like we were *fruits* or *vegetables*!" Like tomatoes, or, or pears!" and she spit out the word a second time, "*Pears*! Is that what they think we are?!" From behind she looked something like a ripened pear, but her round wrinkled face looked more like a rutabaga, ruddy coloured and kind of wrinkled. The owner was watching her from behind his counter at the front as she was saying this. "Yeah, yeah," was all he said. He kept repeating it, even as she was talking, "Yeah, yeah." I took a second empty pot from on top of the coffee machine and switched it with the partially full one. A few drops of hot water fell onto the plate making a loud sizzling noise. I made the switch quickly and poured the cupful that had percolated into the first pot into a styrofoam cup. The sizzling continued for a moment and then faded. I picked up a banana on the way to the check-out. He weighed it and then rang it up. As I was paying, the woman said "Thanks for the free coffee," and he smiled and said you're welcome and then he glanced at me and said "Sorry." At first I thought he was talking about the woman's behaviour, which hadn't really bothered me, and I said "don't worry about it, I'm a writer and this kind of stuff is pretty interesting to me." He smiled again. Then as I was leaving it occurred to me that maybe he meant about having to weigh my banana. Or, maybe he meant about charging me for the coffee after giving one away right in front of me. I was weighing these things in my mind as I left and I noticed that the woman had already walked out the door. As the door closed behind me, she waved and yelled at the owner over her shoulder, "Thanks for the free coffee!" It seemed to me that she always said everything twice. Outside, I adjusted my briefcase and took a sip of the coffee. She looked at me, as though she was sizing me up, her head slightly cocked and then she said, "You gotta dollar?" Just like that, "You gotta dollar?" She was smiling. I said I didn't know. One side of me was starting to feel put out again. First I had to listen to her jabbering away, then she took the last drop of coffee away from me, a paying customer, a *regular*, and then she had the nerve to bug me for a dollar. But the other side of me was kind of curious, and it won over. I decided to give her some money. The only thing was, that I hadn't made it to the bank that day. I knew I had some change, and that I had a two-dollar bill in my pocket, but that was about it. As I was digging through my change purse she said, "You write?" and I was smiling and about to say, "yes," but she continued "You write about the war? You writing to the war office? Sending letters about the war?" It didn't make sense, the Iraq thing had been over for almost a year now. What war? "Sending letters to Duplessis?" she said. And then I caught on. This was no ordinary crank. I suddenly noticed that we were standing in front of Zurich Books, a place that specialises in texts on psychology. Freud, Lacan, Jung, self-help books, books on behavioural disorders, different types of psychoses, the whole thing. I gave her four quarters and she said, "Thank you for the dollar, I hope you can afford it." I was about to reply, "No problem," or something to that effect, but a part of me told me to keep my mouth shut and just leave, so I smiled and took a sip of coffee instead, as a way of covering up, and she cocked her head to one side and with a sly look said "What do you think of the coffee?" I said, it was ok. And she shook her head slowly as if talking to some idiot child and said, "It's not very good, really." She took a sip of hers and then said, "I know a place up the street where the coffee is much better, *and* you can sit down, *and* you can listen to muuusic," and again she stretched out the word, "beeyooteeful muuusic," and for a moment I thought I could see her eyes drift back to Paris, and I began to wonder what it was that she left behind, what it was that made her this way. And then she told me about another coffee shop in the opposite direction. "Also quite good," she said, "...anyway, better than this place." As she said this, I noticed that we were both holding our coffees in our left hands. And I wanted to tell her that, good as those places might be, the price was right at this one. But something inside me made me hold back, and instead I began to think of her as some sort of coffee aficionado, and I could almost picture her, sitting at a circular table on a boulevard, in Paris, sipping coffee, maybe exchanging glances with an accordion player somewhere in the background. But I quickly dismissed the thought, and instead, I said, "thanks for the tip about the coffee." And again, she said, "thank you for the dollar." And we split, and she walked west and I walked east, both of us with our coffees in our hands.

Dear Petrov,

Once again, I write you, and send you questions only. Do they let you out some days? With the family? Or, are you still somewhere on the Ribbentrop line, hiding behind a wall, in the snow, with a Molotov cocktail, waiting for the tanks, the tanks that never come. The snow. Have you ever cracked the valence code? Translated Tellurium, deciphered Antimony? Do you smile raging beneath your skull at the vaticinal sun in the ammonia morning? Or, is this just another "thank-you-ma'am," a bump in the road to alimentotherapeutic recovery? "Rutabega, rutabega, sis-boom bah, simalacrum theory, rah! rah! rah!" Brother... have you cracked? Have you flipped? That last time was too much, taking your mother and father hostage — after they had held you for so long. In some ways it made perfect sense, to me, but the concatenations you made were too much for the Biedermeier blue-coats. You, who read the language of the air, what alterity had you entered? What un-nerved you? Was it some murmuration of starlings that you read as though it were some airborne aria? Or, were you just playing the freebooter, into rapparee, hell-bent on appropriating anything that had not been rendered useless by your macro-cosmic polymythy. I remember you as they trussed you, your exclamations *con brio* before they rendered you costive. Mercurial if impecunious, you charged their noisome presence, their barrels levelled at your heart, your movements terpsichorean, specular, as if you were watching yourself — as if, they were, I was, not there...how could they have known, you were harmless. You raged, darling *enfant terrible*, dyspeptic, drinking your own molotov, an anonym, singing your loud song, inventing your own paroemiology, bellowing out; "When I got out of the cab, when I withdrew from the taxi, all of my clothes were inside out!" You tried to put it off. "Think of a coin. A golden ducat, a piece of silver, a ruble, a Canadian Looney — whatever. Did you know that the CIBC is collecting pennies for Alzheimer's victims?" you said. "Consider an extended zero-gravity condition, the space-shuttle for example. One flips a coin. It spins and spins and never stops, never falls. This is a tough decision, they say. Let's flip a coin, they say." But the cabby wouldn't have any of it. "Pay up or get out," he said. Later, you explained it through Riemannian integrals, poor proverb that it was, "One gets into a cab, forgets his money, forgets where he's going, the cabby protests, one searches one's clothes, thoroughly, one finds no money. Thus, one enters a cab, the cab moves down the boulevard, as it moves, one finds one's condition to be minus one's funds, minus one's destination, minus one's clothes, minus one's mind, the cabby refuses to go further, one speculates upon the situation, naked, a zero, ground zero, destination...zero. Period. One puts one's clothes back on, still without destination, still without coin, yet things have somehow changed." But, you didn't stop there, you walked home, you sang, raged. Later, I watched, a dumb fool, observing breathless, as though at a peepshow, your Aria; "How does the tiger-lily, lean against a lean-to? Ma! Paw! Tiger! Lily! White! Wedding! Bells! Ring! Neck! Peasant!" You sang — I cowered in the crowd, was cowed and listened, but failed to intervene, not that it would've mattered, your song had to be sung, even as they trussed you, pushed you into the cruiser, "a door, opens," you sang, "adore, oh! pense!" they pushed you in, "adoro penso!" I still remember, I do remember.

I received your last letter, and I thank you for your words. Do you remember the things you said? "A horse is a *steed* or *charger*. The enemy is *the foe* or *the host*. Danger is *peril*. Actions are *deeds*. To die is to *perish*. To show cowardice is *to swerve*. Nothing is *naught*. Nothing but, is *naught, save*. One's chest is *one's breast*. Sleep is *slumber*. The objective is *the goal*. One's death is *one's fate*. Things that glow or shine are *radiant*. The blood of young men is *the red sweet wine of youth*. The corpse constitutes *ashes or dust*. A friend is *a comrade*. To die is *to swerve*. To sleep is *one's fate*. The objective is *naught*. Danger is *radiant*. Slumber is *the goal*. The breast is naught *save the host*." I do remember. Today, I read some words by Bergson, perhaps you remember? "— the rigid, the ready-made, the mechanical, in contrast with the supple, the ever-changing and the living, absentmindedness in contrast with attention, such are the defects that laughter singles out and would fain correct." it was part of a page in a book that I was photocopying, I was copying many pages...automaton-like...until I felt like some sort of servo-mechanism, each page became a Riemannian integer, a copy, minus one degree of sensibility, a copy minus one plus one degrees of sensibility, a copy minus one plus one plus one degrees of sensibility, and so on. Somehow, I thought this might amuse you.

Your friend,

Karl

P.S. As you know, dear Petrov, the Riemannian integral is a definite integral defined as the limit of sums found by partitioning the interval comprising the domain of definition into subintervals, by finding the sum of products each of which consists of the width or a subinterval multiplied by the value of the function at some point in it, and by letting the maximum width of the subintervals approach zero. Consider Zeno's arrow. Consider two mirrors facing each other, with yourself in between. This can become a speculation of alterity to the Nth degree. Now place that coin in zero gravity, flipping between those mirrors. Do you remember the barber shop?

P.P.S. I am enclosing a box of your favourite cigars.

Ashes, ashes

The fire begins late afternoon, not long after her daughter leaves. Leaves, having forgotten to turn off the oven with the bread still in it. The acrid odour, like scorched toast, is the first indication. And the smoke. The old woman watches it stream, at first faintly, from the cracks around the oven door, rise and billow upward where it diffuses slowly, spreading a dull veil below the ceiling. Wisps of it twine around the white and green leaves of the ivy she loves, then float toward the window, left slightly open.

"Mother, don't close the window so tight," her daughter always says. "I nearly choke in this place. You need air. Leave it open a crack, like this."

In the gathering smoke the woman's clouded eyes can no longer distinguish clearly the familiar objects on the table: the picture of her daughter, a pile of folded paper serviettes, used but too good to throw away, wool socks and mittens, the magnifying glass without which she is blind.

Her joints, disfigured and rampant with arthritis, feel stiffer than usual and she can't summon the will to move them. She coughs, closes her burning eyes.

"Don't turn the oven on, Mother. Ever." Her daughter repeats and repeats these words whenever she comes. Comes in a bustle of energy and words and movements too quick to comprehend. And then leaves. "If you must bake, do it when I'm here." But it is the daughter who has forgotten to turn off the oven. The old woman is certain of that.

The thickening smoke cannot be shut out. Her coughing increases. And she feels warm. But it is not the comforting warmth her flesh and bones crave, not the warmth that might relieve the excruciating pain and cold. Lately her feet and hands are never warm. "Wear socks. Wear wool mittens," her daughter says, rummaging through drawers. She places a pair of each neatly on the bedside table before she leaves. "Wear them to bed."

The woman tries to remember, but invariably she wakes around midnight, her feet and hands icy, the mittens she had intended to wear beyond her reach on the table. She is so stiff she can't move and only the ingrained habit of will prevents her from screaming out her fear. Those are the worst hours. The hours between midnight and dawn. The hours of sleepless immobility. The dead silence.

Around the smoke-swathed oven, tiny flames reach out, leaping in all directions.

Let's say the old woman imagines the fire creeping along the floor, playing gently around her feet. The crepe soles of her shoes shrink, the leather turns dark. Her cotton stockings resist the flames with more success than her blue flowered polyester dress, which shrivels quickly and is gone. Her cotton underwear will not fend off the remorseless incision of the flames. Her wispy white hair will be singed, her skin scorched black.

Is it possible that the pain holding the woman, day after day in its implacable grip can be driven out by a greater, more terrible pain? Does fire sear and purify?

Let's say she wants to call out her daughter's name, but the name is gone. Not only the body, but also the mind betrays.

Who can say for certain what images of inevitable horror push their way, against her terrible will, into her nebulous mind and mingle there with her tenuous memories. Let's say the terror gathers there, and forces out from her very centre a brilliant outcry. It melts into the roar of the flames, this outcry, and becomes one with the agonised scream of the siren.

The sound carries into the universe. It is the only thing left when everything has turned to ashes.

The Roommate

The tour was a success and Dagmar was glad she'd come. True, the olive trees in Gethsemane were gnarled, ugly things, the Jordan River a dreary, insignificant stream — even Winnipeg's Red River was more imposing — and she became weary of smelly camels, weary of fending off scruffy Arab children who moved in swarms and pushed painted beads into her hands. Still, this was where Jesus had lived, had walked and eaten bread, had welcomed children, healed the sick, even raised the dead.

Daily the afternoon light blessed the stone buildings of Jerusalem with a rose glow. The beautiful city set on hills. They had crossed the Sea of Galilee on a beautiful day, no hint of the sudden storms all Bible commentaries mention; and the Mount of Beatitudes cradled on its slope a hollow so natural she could imagine the crowd nestled in it, listening, rapt, while Jesus admonished his disciples: "You are the salt of the earth. You are the light of the world."

But there was the problem of her roommate. The travel agent in Winnipeg had assured her that Mrs. Reimer, the elderly Mennonite woman from Gnadenfeld, would be an ideal companion, but this had clearly been a deception designed to spare Mrs. Reimer the cost of a single room.

Dagmar couldn't imagine how Mrs. Reimer spent her share of time in the bathroom. She was never quite clean, washed her grey, tightly-permed hair only once in three weeks, you'd almost think she feared water. Day after day she wore the same flowered skirt with one change of blouse. She jabbered constantly, her flat vowels and faulty verb tenses a jarring assault on Dagmar's sensibility. Worst of all, she trailed Dagmar like a shadow, reminding her, "Vee are partners. Vee valk together vere Jesus been."

Dagmar, although she preferred to keep to herself, made careful efforts to get acquainted with other group members, and when the group entered a restaurant, she could count on a beckoning hand somewhere. No one ever raised a beckoning hand for Mrs. Reimer. On the bus, Dagmar learned never to sit beside a vacant seat that her roommate would inevitably occupy.

At the Dead Sea, the soft flesh of her thighs and shoulders swelling from an apple-green bathing suit, Mrs. Reimer followed Dagmar to the water's edge. Dagmar had read that the sea did not only contain salt, but also an abundance of sulphurous and nitrous chemicals and she wasn't surprised that it felt thick and oily around her ankles. "Vait!" The querulous fear in Mrs. Reimer's cry stopped Dagmar. She turned, unwillingly, just in time to see her roommate stumble, fall forward, face down in the shallow water. A moan bubbled up from the mound of flesh in the apple-green bathing suit, as it settled into the muddy sea. There was a final lurch triggered by a sort of gasping suction, as if a giant sponge was absorbing everything.

After some confusion and with the help of the tour guide and a burly tourist, Mrs. Reimer was heaved and hoisted out, helped to a stone ledge away from the water. Shaking, she put her hand to her mouth, pulled out her denture which she set on the stone ledge beside her, and sat coughing, vomiting out a surprising quantity of grey bile.

That evening when they were getting ready for bed, Mrs. Reimer had nothing to say. As usual there was no long sound of bath water running from faucet or shower while she was in the bathroom, and although tonight Dagmar listened for muffled sobbing, she could hear none.

When she emerged in her crumpled nightgown, her mouth empty of its denture, her face grey, Mrs. Reimer said, "I vos nearly dead out dere." She turned off her night light and crawled into bed.

Dagmar took out her journal, found a comfortable upright position in bed, and sat a while, lost in thought. Then she wrote: *April 21: A beautiful summer day. We all went swimming in the Dead Sea in which you can float because of the salt. But no living things survive in the water, and even the birds, I've read, avoid flying over it.*

Then she too turned off her light, pulled the sheet over herself like a shroud and buried her head in the pillow.

The Ice Cream Cake

The woman in the elevator wants to give me half a watermelon. She shows me its cut side, coral-red, speckled with small black seeds. She wants me to have it. She tells me this in spite of the fact that she speaks no English, I no Lithuanian. Her small daughter grins and dances on her toes in the half-light of the descending elevator. The white gauze ribbon poised like a fat butterfly on top of her head trembles.

I've said No to the woman. I'm going to the Pinguin ice cream store, a block from the hotel, where a cake is waiting for me. An ice cream cake which I've ordered for my friends, who are foreigners here like myself. We'll eat it on the balcony of the hotel at ten o'clock when the sun is a dull-red sphere sinking into the misty horizon, somewhere beyond the northwest fringe of the city.

The street is still filled with the soft light of evening. The woman is at my elbow. She takes my arm and offers me a cigarette. Impatient, I shake my head, No, I don't smoke. She motions left with her arm, but I motion ahead toward the Pinguin store. She would much rather go left, but only if I come with her. Her small daughter is skipping along the sidewalk, casting a long shadow. She avoids the cracks.

In the Pinguin store there's a queue, but not as long as usual. The woman steps ahead of me. She orders ice cream in three old-fashioned, footed ice cream dishes. I grab her arm and say, No, and shake my head repeatedly, but she is unshakable. She smiles and tells me we'll eat the ice cream at one of the small round tables near the window.

There are three scoops of ice cream in each pewter dish. One is strawberry-pink, one lime-green, and one the colour of melon. The woman sets down the bag with the half-watermelon on the table beside her. She offers me a cigarette. I shake my head. She tells me she's from the city of Kaunas. She already knows that I'm from Canada. She's telling me why she and her daughter are here in the same hotel where I'm staying with my friends, but I can't understand her. The sun's low rays pour in through the dusty window.

When I've eaten the strawberry-pink ice cream, part of the lime-green and a bite of the melon, I tell the woman I must go. Her eyes are uncomprehending. When I rise, she stubs out her cigarette and rises too, and so does her small daughter whose name is Audra. They follow me to the counter where there's only one person ahead of me, a man with a plastic container he wants filled with scoops of ice cream, vanilla and raspberry.

When it's my turn, I form a large round circle with my hands, the shape of a cake, and pronounce the name of my hotel. The girl behind the counter disappears behind a door and when she returns with my cake, the woman at my elbow speaks to her in Lithuanian, the words rippling from her tongue like beads, quickly, ungently. The girl disappears again and comes with a second cake. The woman wants me to have it.

I make it very clear that I don't need to two cakes, that it's impossible for me to accept another cake. But she's already paying for it.

We leave the Pinguin store each carrying a cake, the woman slightly behind me, chattering constantly in her language. The bag with the half-watermelon hangs from the woman's left wrist. Beside her, Audra walks with the tiniest of steps, laughing, chanting a child's verse and avoiding the cracks.

At the hotel we join the crowd waiting to enter the elevator. I push my way into the packed, stifling cavity. When I turn around, the doors are already closing.

At ten o'clock the sun sets. Bit by bit its dull, round flaming slides into the darkness that is the city's edge. We watch from the railing of the balcony and eat thin slices of ice cream cake. The last crack of light disappears, leaving a coral glow. The view is perfect.

I can see with incredible clarity the wide-brown, alarmed eyes of the woman. She extends both arms toward me, offering the cake. The strap of the bag containing the half-watermelon cuts deeply into her left wrist.

Standing perfectly still beside her is Audra, eyes round and very sombre. A slice of filmy white ribbon is the last thing I see through the narrowing crack of the elevator doors.

Order

Ricky Kruse always came to class before the others, eagerly. It had very little to do with Mathematics or Eileen Roscoe, the teacher, though he had no objection to either. Already he was spreading the pictures of Elvis neatly on his desk, which was in the centre of the classroom. There were faded newspaper clippings, glossy photographs, a colour blow-up showing the King in concert, legs spread, eyes closed, an explosion of stage lights framing his fierce ecstasy. Ricky placed each picture thoughtfully, moved it here, there a half-inch, arranging and rearranging everything with obvious intention until the display was perfectly ordered. The fact that the order was fragile, that it could be destroyed, by accident or deliberately, did not seem to trouble him.

Then he drew his awkward shoulders straight, settled back into the desk which was too small and laid his huge hands gently on either side of the pictures. His ruddy face softened, the pimply forehead relaxed, and a kind of peace spread over his countenance.

Eileen Roscoe came to her Math 201 class straight from the staff room, as usual. Over coffee and a cigarette she had followed the conversation as she always did, without actually entering it. Ricky Kruse was a real nut case, they said. In Geography he'd broken into tears, can you believe it, when someone took his favourite magazine picture of Elvis. Ricky Kruse's mother was mad as the moon. Walked in front of traffic at the mall, expecting drivers to stop for her. The old man had finally left her, good riddance, after roaring through the house one day leaving disaster in his wake. Had everyone noticed Ricky's bruises were fading, no new ones lately. Eileen Roscoe was always amazed at the information to be gained, information that others acquired from who knows what source, long before it occurred to her to inquire. She put off telling Ricky to clear his desk, this was Math class. Ricky was not a trouble-maker and anyway she stood a bit in awe of his acquaintance with the elements of worship: order, this reverent silence and, for all she knew, a pure heart. It could be worse. She'd once had a student who'd threatened to blow up the world.

The students of Math 201 held off entering the class until the last minute. They did not like mathematics, nor the teacher. This was nothing personal, just a circumstance.

They straggled in, finally, the teacher chanting: hurry up hurry move now nice shirt Darcy no Elizabeth you can't get your books you should have them with you Megan before you get too comfy let's have that essay on Robert Frost due let me remind you not yesterday but last week.

And the students: You've got to move me Miss R the desk's broken Miss R are we doing anything today piss off willya Bernstedt ya scum hi Miss Roscoe who ripped off the unicorn poster hey Ricky baby how's Graceland.

It was Jennifer who bumped against Ricky's desk today, Jennifer who was not ungraceful, just unmindful. A book slid from her arms onto the altar before which Ricky sat in silent adoration, and suddenly everything was in disarray.

Pictures floated to the aisle where they were stepped on. The students who first noticed the disruption laughed loudly, exaggeratedly, and the derision caught hold, spreading like a wave through the class. Someone's arm swept away the entire display. Jennifer was jostled to her desk, her small sorry sorry Rick lost in the pandemonium.

Held by the transformation on Ricky Kruse's face where all peace was shattered, Eileen Roscoe hesitated. Firmness was called for, words, actions to restore order. But she said nothing, her attention fixed on Ricky, who seemed to grow even larger, more awkward, as he pulled himself upright, hands gripping the desk edge. She watched his lips part, his mouth open and from somewhere deep within came not so much a scream as a bellow that swelled and swelled filling the room.

The class fell quiet, shocked, silenced by the sound. All eyes were fixed on Eileen Roscoe. This was a moment to be taken advantage of, the silence an opportunity to be seized. But for what? There was more to be restored than class order, more than a ravaged icon. The chaos torn from inside Ricky Krause lay naked before them.

Eileen Roscoe stood a long while, irresolute. When at last she moved her wooden hands to pick up, woodenly, the Math text on her desk, it was as heavy as stone, heavy as the dead-weight inside her. Turn to page 87, she said, let's review the acute and obtuse angles. Ricky had shrunk, slumped down in his desk, drawn into himself, snail-like. Near the back, Jennifer sat quietly crying.

This Morning We Killed a Man, and This is How it Happened

Today, this very morning, we killed Bob Dick and stole his horses. Damn good horses, too. They was almost worth it. We come up the lake shore walkin' on the sand. It was about a mile from pa's old place and the sand was froze a little, which was quite strange for this early in the fall. Bob was still in bed so we was just going to take his horses and skedaddle. Trouble was Bob's hired man Jake Tooney was waitin' there with a loaded gun like he was expectin' us. I ain't absolutely too sure, but somebody must have tipped him to the fact that we was comin'. He didn't say nothin'. Just shot Tommy Martin in the ear. How a man can manage to make any kind of sound when his brains is hove in I don't know, but Tommy fell crowin' and whistlin' like a bird in a snake fight.

None of us knew he was dead till Jimmy Hyde screamed, "J-j-j-jesus H. C-c-c-christ. T-t-t-tommy's d-d-d-dead." And then we all seen the blood come leakin' out from under his head like a busted rum jug.

Jake Tooney run in the house and we made quick for cover except John Dickson who never seemed afraid of nothin'. He just walked over to the barn, unlatched the door and in five minutes come out with the two fine geldings of Bob Dick's bridled and ready to go.

We was all layin' low as dogs in the shade when Bob come racketing out onto the porch.

"You lead them horses back where you go them, Mister."

John Dickson just smiled. He has a way of smilin' that says the same as when other men spit. I could see pa out of the corner of my eye. He was lyin' very still, taking a bead on Robert Dick. It reminded me of how still pa could be when he wanted to be. I'm pretty certain pa was waitin' for some sign that Robert Dick was worth killin' when somebody else shot him right on the word Mr.. Anyways, whoever it was made a mess of his face. He crashed back into the door and gargled blood for a whole minute before he expired. John Dickson never stopped smilin'. He just turned around and walked away like he'd trick-traded for them horses. Pa eased the hammer of his piece and stutterin' Jimmy Hyde he whimpered like he was a dog locked in a gutting shed.

We buried both corpses in the same grave. It looked a little like they was huddled together to keep out the cold. Pa said he'd had enough and he left the country and I never seen him again. Funny thing about that business. They never tried any of us for the murder of Robert Dick. And both of them horses died from pneumonia. And I heard how Jake Tooney fell in the creek and drowned. When they found him he had a fish hook in both of his eyes. My guess is, he must have been using the wrong kind of bait.

The Boy With a Duck on His Head

The boy is five, running for the farmhouse with a duck on his head. The duck is flapping his wings, beating the boy's ears, hauling at his scalp like a storm shingle hiking its nails. The boy is running, the duck on his head gyrating like a tin roof half torn off, the bill drinking blood. The boy is running, his mad hands flashing like a feather plucker in the belly down, the duck cleated so the toe webs are stretched open and rubbery, adhering to the flesh below the hair. The boy is running for the farmhouse where his grandfather is at the gate jacking the manure from his boots, first one, then the other, so the sheep dung is there on the jack blade whickered with straw, and dark green, lincoln green, cud green, apple-shit green, a high sweet rose-garden stink instant and to be relished. The grandfather says nothing. With his eyes says, "Don't hurt that duck, boy." Says, "Ducks are money." With his eyes. Turns. Walks towards the house. Leaves the boy with the duck on his head like a living hat.

The Day the Devil Come to Highgate

Once a troupe of black evangelists come to the village. One fella preached till he got so hot steam come rollin' out through his shirt. Well, I never did go in much for hell-fire and brimstone, so when I heard him conjurin' the worst of Revelations, and them choir girls got to wild-eyed weepin' and gnashin' their teeth like horses in Gomorrah, I come up with a plan.

I snuck into the Highgate hotel where they was stayin' and secreted myself under one of them black women's beds before she got back. Now, I swear I never peeked once while she tinkled the comode. And I hardly breathed when the springs sagged down and touched my belly. It took her half hour or more to get settled, but when she got to sawin' logs real steady like she was buildin' a fence, I took a good holt of that iron bed frame and shook it till it bucked like a heifer snubbed for getting her horns cut. Well she jumped up screechin' and hollerin', "It's da debil! It's da debil!"

The preachers here have quit preaching hell. The Reverend Cross, and Canon Smith both. But the book of thought is never closed. What people believed then, whatever they believe now — it was worth spendin' a night or two in jail just to hear that woman screechin' "It's da debil, it's da debil." That was sixty years ago when the Prince of Darkness come to Highgate.

Herb Lee's Tweed Suit

Woot Hardy made me a beautiful tweed suit. He made me three pairs of pants at fifty cents a pair. An awful price for pants. Highway robbery. But they was tailored best in the country. I even had my picture took in them duds. I was gallused and gussied up like a city lawyer. I coulda' robbed any simple farmer in the country and they'd of called it justice long as I was wearin' them clothes and I wore them clothes back in the days when I was runnin' cattle and sheep from the old country.

I was over to London stayin' at a hotel in a room I shared with a fella named Mr. O'Leary. A real friendly guy. He could oil his hands without touchin' his hair. A good talker. We did have some pretty high times. Well, when he got sight o' that suit, I swear you'd a thought I was the King of England.

"Oh that's one fine suit you have there, Herb," he'd say rubbin' his hands like they were frost bit. "Oh my that cloth — so richly woven," he'd say, "so finely cut," he'd say, "so stylish, yet so serviceable," his voice smooth as peeled plums. It was like he was tryin' to sell me my own suit the way he went on, touchin' the material like it was wove with gold. I guess I should have suspected somethin', but I didn't, cause I thought we were friends.

Anyways, I always sleep in the raw and when morning come and I went to get my suit from the closet there weren't nothin' there but O'Leary's shape. He'd left me his own cheap, shrunk down stuff and high-tailed it like a dog with kitchen scraps. I felt about like a pawn-broker's best customer puttin' my long limbs in them short pants. I had four inches of white calf to spare and my arms come out of the sleeves like one of them performin' circus monkeys. I could'a washed myself wrist to elbow and not dampened the twill. It musta looked as if I'd grown in the night. If I'd of flexed my shoulders I'd of split a stitch in the coat, collar to tail.

Needless to say I was ready to kill O'Leary if I ever saw him again. I ate breakfast and went about my business cause I had things to do. Well if I didn't catch sight of that same Mr. O'Leary comin' on real loose and dandy in my fine tweeds, and me lookin' like hard times come in the wrong size. I was kind of waitin' for him to see me and then I'd call him out, right there in the street. Sure enough he caught sight of me, but instead of jumpin' back in the doorway the way I expected he kept on comin' smilin' like he owned the street.

He come right by me and says, "Good morning, Mr. O'Leary," tippin' his hat like a tea cup tilted to look for dregs. I had to check myself twice to be certain I was still Herb. That son of a bitch had on my Woot Hardy tailored suit and he was tryin' on my name as if he believed the clothes really do make the man, or then when they fail, words will do the trick as well.

I didn't do nothin'. Just stood there my jaw slack as if the hinge had lost its bite, hand gangly in my coat as if the dirt couldn't quite keep the root. I be damned if there weren't two Mr. O'Learys and two Herb Lees right there in the streets of London and I just stood there tryin' to get it straight in my mind which one was wearin' whose suit.

The Lamb Killing

When you're killing lamb you wait for the cold, or else the meat will spoil. Three days of certain cold. If the ice melts on the cattle trough, you're scuppered. A sudden thaw — you're done. If the window glass is ever hot enough to fool the winter flies into getting born, if the sunlight butters the snow till it steams like January, well you might as well gut the lamb for cats. In them days before freezers there was an art to the kill.

Stella used to boil the meat and jar it like an apricot crop. Lay the hogs in salt. Cook a heifer and leave her so she sinks cut-up in her own fat like cheese in cool cream.

After you've killed — you spread the hind legs open like the jaws of a broken-hinged trap and thread the gambrel through the thews just above the hoof, then hook a clevis in the centre ring and hang the carcass so it spins a little half-turn like a kid in a swing. Then you get to work and cut off the head.

If the weather holds — you don't have nothin' left to bury.

Emeralds

She left him eleven months after her arrival leaving an infant and a khaki skirt with a torn pocket. It was the same one she had worn when she arrived at the farm with her arm around his uniformed waist. A war bride awaiting the open spaces and streaked sunsets.

He had met her in a London museum standing in front of a display of sailing ships, her hair wrapped in a bandana as if awaiting an unexpected wind. She told him of her love for the sea. They were married in a small church near her flat. He said it would be forever because God did not arrange chance meetings without intent.

His sister met them at the railway station and did not shake her hand but rather picked up his suitcase instead. The farm was not coloured as he had described. The front step was a gray boulder that would not catch the brown dirt from the barn.

That winter the cold seeped through her at nights forcing the child inside her to roll in a ball of constant pain. His sister scoffed at his pamperings . . . starting the fires before his wife put her feet to the floor and the making of extra cups of tea with canned milk.

In July they called for the most expensive midwife, and the girl was born under a sailor's moon. He named her Lena, after his mother.

She left the farm and the country two days after the first winter storm covered the lilac bushes. He knew she was gone when he returned from town with the Carnation milk she had requested. He took the stairs to their bedroom three at a time. His sister was standing at the foot of the bed holding the child. "I've moved Lena's cradle into my room," she said.

Bingo

We figured that Basil and Betty must have been conceived during a blue moon or a hailstorm or something. They were twins and completely opposite and not just because of being a girl and a boy. Basil was a small baby with red hair and blue eyes. Betty was three and a half pounds heavier with black hair.

It was obvious from the time Basil could crawl he was special. He was his father's man-to-be. His father was Carl Smith, the county postmaster. Carl was a quiet man as solid as the oak desk in his office. He didn't marry until after his mother died, too late to even bother some people said. Carl was forty-seven when the twins were born, and he and the wife went foolish trying to look after them.

After Basil was off the bottle, Carl would take him to the post office in the afternoons to give his wife a break. Anytime you'd pick up your mail after lunch, Basil would be there crawling around the floor mimicking everything he heard. A happy kid. Carl would add up the cost of stamps or parcels with a pencil and paper, talking out loud as he did it. Then something strange started happening. Basil began calling out the answers before Carl had a chance to get the numbers on the paper. Now the morning people waited till Basil got there before they picked up their mail just to test the kid. There was a writeup in the *Chronicle* about Basil being a genius. It was even suggested that he should go to some special school in the States, but Carl wouldn't hear of it.

Basil and Betty started grade one together, only Basil read with the grade sixes. After school the bus would let him off at the post office to sit on the counter adding and subtracting numbers like a machine gun. Sometimes when enough people had gathered, Carl would close the post office and carry Basil out back to the shed door he had painted black. Then he'd take a chunk of white chalk and put high numbers down in squares just like a Bingo card. Someone would point to a line, and Basil would shout the answer before we could get it checked on the paper.

Carl took the kid everywhere even to the Legion on Saturdays. Basil would sit on his father's lap and watch us play. It got so he could tell his father what cards was left in the pack.

In the fall, the principal told Carl that Basil should to go the city school where he could get even smarter. Carl said he would think about it, but he didn't have to. In August, Basil got sick with pains. Carl nursed him through the night. The next day they took him to the hospital, but it was too late because his appendix had split open and poisoned him to death.

Carl was pretty good at the funeral, we thought, until Fred told us he heard a racket later that night. Fred looked out and saw Carl shooting the hell out of the black door behind the post office. Fred said he kept loading the shotgun and blasting it till there was nothing left.

Betty missed grade three.

Her Mother's Brother

He comes up the stairs walking on the steps next to the wallpaper where the wood doesn't creak. He has this down to a science. The mother is sleeping in the bedroom across the hall, the left side of her bed empty as if she expects her dead husband to crawl in before dawn.

He opens the door to the girl's bedroom and closes it softly. The girl winces and doubles up like a slapped caterpillar curling into a ball to shut him out. He is on his knees pulling her gently from the wall. His axe handle hands pry her open. He whispers softly as he pulls the nightie over her braids.

The Hourglass

John Gillis had a 1940 Lincoln Zepher. It was a true possession. He was polishing it when he heard about Clyde being killed by a train. Marion had come out to the garage to say that Clyde and the car were unrecognisable. She repeated all the details the way people do when they sense the power of relating a horror.

"He was dragged sixty feet," she said. "Before the train cut everything including Clyde in half. A nine-year-old boy saw the whole thing."

Marion moved to the side of the car John was working on. "Sylvia was at the church (choir night) with the two girls when she heard. Clyde's hand was still holding a package of cigarettes (Players) when they found the top half of him." John heard the details again each time the phone rang after supper.

Clyde Matthews had been John's best friend for twenty years. After high school they had opened a small garage together, John fixing the cars and Clyde doing the books. In the fall of fifty-three Clyde met Sylvia Thompson at the Riverbend dance hall. Her father owned the Lakewood Lumber Company in Moncton, and that's where they moved after they married. Clyde joined the company and went into sales where it was said he could sell a car without wheels for profit.

John and Marion were married the month Sylvia had a baby girl, so Clyde couldn't make it to their wedding. John called to congratulate him on his daughter. Clyde laughed and said it wasn't something to be patted on the back for. "Making a girl is easy," he said. "The pattern's right there in front of you." John laughed. "It's a boy I want," said Clyde. "I want something named after me."

John didn't see much of Clyde after he married. Moncton wasn't that far away, but Marion and Sylvia didn't "get along" as they say. Marion had heard that Sylvia suggested Marion always wore lyle stockings because of varicose veins. Sylvia wore nylons.

It snowed the day of Clyde's funeral, not enough to keep cars off the road, but enough to excuse them for staying in a garage. Marion had made a donation to Clyde's church instead of sending an arrangement. "Flowers were a waste," she said. "Just a big show."

That night John went to the garage and raised the hood of his twelve cylinder engine. He hooked the trouble light to the horn bracket and took a carbide stamp from his pocket. He carefully tapped the initials C E M into the block of the engine. It was the best he could do.

The Button

His family said Marven Banister was trying to shoot a raven when he accidentally killed himself. We all knew it was the second marriage that had turned the gun muzzle to his head and not to the trees. And what would a fisherman be doing with a gun at a rented cottage anyway.

There was no question that she had driven him to it with her adjuratums and marigolds planted in a perfect B, on the lawn. They say the second one is always a copy of the first, but Marven's first wife gardened with an eye to the freezer, stocking it with strawberries, beans, peas and blueberries; she baked her own bread and was a member of the Ladies Auxilliary.

This one monogrammed the damned lawn and kept nail polish in the fridge. Bill Small saw it there the days he delivered their eggs, bottles lined up along a whole shelf on the door. She bought square bread and cut the crusts off throwing the goodness out to feed the birds. She joined the curling club without her husband and learned to draw perfectly to the circle. She even made the playoffs last year.

Too bad some of that good aiming hadn't rubbed off on Marven.

May 24th Weekend

Lilac bushes here. One hundred Shasta Daisies filling the space behind the garage. Trudy gazed out the window, planning the garden while they waited for all danger of frost to pass. A sheet of graph paper was spread out on the kitchen table in front of her. Mock Orange beside the deck. Bleeding Hearts in the southwest corner where the sun was strongest. Two apple trees, one to pollinate the other.

The time came to plant. Reg had already turned their compost into the earth, which was drunk with melted snow and spring rains. Trudy perched on the deck watching Reg slide the spade into the loamy soil. He was digging the hole for the second apple tree when Trudy stood up and felt a sudden gush. She reached a hand between her legs and it came up bright red. Then she felt a searing pain followed by the first, breathtaking contraction.

By the time the ambulance arrived it was all over. Trudy demanded to see the fetus. At 13 weeks it was too small and inviolable even to hold its shape. She thought of the miraculous in vitro photographs she'd studied in such detail. Fetuses sucking their thumbs, swimming somersaults. Her own child had done all that and more. She'd seen it smile and crawl and take its first tottering steps. She'd kissed its skinned knees and arranged the daisies it plucked into a glass vase on the kitchen table. She'd watched it climb the apple trees and laugh at her fears.

The doctors wanted to do tests. Find out why. She agreed, but only if they'd give it back to her afterwards. It was a girl. That's all they discovered.

Of course there was no funeral, no cards, no flowers. "You'll have another," said well-meaning friends, those who had the courage to say anything at all.

A few days later she left the hospital with the fetus in a plastic bag like a piece of liver from the supermarket. She and Reg buried it in the hole meant for the apple tree.

That night the skies erupted in a thunderstorm that shook the foundations of their house. Trudy ran outside to lay a small flannel blanket over the fresh mound of earth.

The World

The Middle East is crushed. There is a gash, a split stretching from Moscow down through Turkey, Israel, Egypt and the Sudan almost to Uganda. It's not very big, only about the size of a grapefruit and it's hollow inside. She can see through the layers of cardboard to the darkness. It makes her think of the holes she used to dig in her backyard, convinced she would reach China in a single afternoon. There's a big dent in China, which is orange on this globe. The mountain ranges have turned into craters.

Her kids have never tried to dig to China. They don't believe in the Tooth Fairy or Santa Claus. They're not smug about it, they just don't believe in those things. Maxine had been the one to ask her. At first she'd hedged, trying to determine whether or not she really wanted to know. Maxine had gone and told the others who accepted it very matter-of-factly. Not that they were lacking in imagination. Rachel believed in the Care Bears. She confided to Heather that Lucky Bear had blinked at her from the shelf in her bedroom. And Maxine still half-believed that she might one day fly.

Forgetting the unwashed breakfast dishes, the unvacuumed carpet, the unmade beds, she examines this damaged globe retrieved from under the couch. Slipping a bread and butter knife into the Black Sea, she gently pokes and prods underneath the surface of China, trying to elevate the mountains without widening the gap. It's delicate work, and she finds herself growing angry. It's not as though they don't have plenty of balls to play with. Why do they have to use this? She doubts whether any one of them could locate Canada without difficulty. Outside the window squirrels are scurrying through the unraked leaves, filling their cheeks. She pauses for a moment to watch them, then returns to this task which absorbs her completely until the lunch-time flurry of peanut butter sandwiches and spilled milk, arguments over who gets which cup and who gets the last cookie, or the biggest *piece* of the last cookie. The children are oblivious to her sour mood.

"God is everywhere," David announces soberly, out of nowhere. "Even in the air."

"And inside you, too," says Rachel.

"He's in your nose," Maxine adds with a sniff. The others giggle. "and in your belly button and between your toes and in your bum!"

As soon as they leave for school, Heather goes back to work on the globe, but she is no longer confident of her ability to restore it. She is aware of the silence that the children have left in their wake, a silence which threatens to swallow her up. Soon she will do the dishes and start dinner. She tosses the globe in the garbage. When her husband asks her what she did today, she won't know what to tell him.

Salad Days

Pee that's dried on hardwood leaves a white stain. Pee that's dried on vinyl flooring is sticky and must be washed several times with soap and water to be entirely removed. Pee that's rinsed out of clothing with clear water and no soap will stink when it dries on the shower curtain rod in the bathroom.

Molly suspects Doc of licking his own pee. She can smell it on his breath. She finds herself wondering if this is sufficient grounds for having a dog put to sleep.

Joey is five months old. Molly doesn't mind changing diapers. It's a breeze compared to mopping up pee that is not contained in diapers.

Molly is dressing to go out to give a speech on fundraising, when Alma prances into her bedroom stark-naked. She steps on Molly's scale and empties her bladder.

This is by no means the first time she's pulled something like this in the past five months. Molly has always responded patiently with comments such as: "Well, accidents happen," and "I guess you were laughing so hard you couldn't hold it." But this time, seeing the pee gushing over the sides of her scale, she lets loose a flood of invective. Storming into Joey's room, she grabs a diaper and puts it on Alma, who struggles wildly.

"It isn't comfy, Mummy!"

"What do you suggest I do?" Molly demands. "I don't want pee all over my house!"

Molly fastens the tapes. She refuses to take the diaper off until Alma promises to remember to use the toilet next time. Then Molly hugs her, kisses her goodbye, and goes off to speak with authority to a roomful of arts administrators about creative approaches to fundraising.

Later, during Joey's 2:00 a.m. feeding, Molly is startled from her drowsy reverie by the patter of Doc's footsteps on the stairs. She tucks Joey back in his crib and goes downstairs to investigate. She mops up the puddle on the kitchen floor and heads back to bed.

Sometime before dawn she stirs: Doc again, on the stairs. In the morning she plunges barefoot into a puddle on the dining-room floor. Half the furniture has to be moved in order to clean it up. A solution of vinegar and water is supposed to remove the odour. Molly's house smells like salad dressing.

Alma sits at the table, a bowl of Cheerios in front of her, untouched.

Holding Doc's jaw with one hand so the dog can't avoid her eyes, Molly hisses: "If you ever do that again you're gone."

Alma crawls under the table to pat the dog. "Do you love Doc?" she asks.

"No."

Alma sighs heavily.

"Doc is only a dog," Molly adds. "You're my daughter. It doesn't matter what you do. I'll always love you."

Alma finishes her Cheerios, uses the toilet, and Molly drives her to preschool. When she returns, she nurses Joey. As she is putting him down in his crib, Doc enters the room panting heavily and pees on the floor, narrowly missing Molly's foot. She can't even yell because she doesn't want to awaken Joey.

Doc's pee smells not of ammonia but of something hot, pungent, fresh and entirely deliberate.

That night Molly's husband neglects to flush the toilet. Molly lies awake, contemplating divorce.

Pockets

Esther's mother was off at a four-day conference of physiotherapists. Esther was happy to see her go. Not that she didn't like her mother. She did. But she liked assuming the household responsibilities, especially now that she could drive. Chores that she resented when her mother was home offered, in her absence, a taste of autonomy. At sixteen she was quite content to be a housewife when she grew up, although she wouldn't admit this to a soul. With marks like hers she could be whatever she chose. The world, as her father was fond of saying, was her oyster, though oysters struck her as rather cold and unyielding; when pried open they revealed a mysterious fleshy core that may or may not contain a pearl.

Esther was more than happy to pick up the cleaning. Her mother had left her the keys to the Audi. As she pulled up to the cleaner's she debated what to make for dinner. Last night her father had grabbed a bite to eat at the hospital. He'd offered to take her out tonight, but she preferred to cook him a proper meal. Those were the words she'd used — a proper meal. It made her feel competent, nurturing, a good housewife. Chicken, she thought. *Shake 'n Bake*; her father would like that.

She paid for the cleaning, carefully counting out the exact change from the cash her mother had left for her. The cleaner's policy was to place anything found in the clothing in envelopes designed to look like pockets, complete with *faux* buttons with which the envelopes could be sealed. Strung from the hanger containing her father's suit was one such envelope.

Esther put the chicken in the oven and set the table before she put the cleaning away. It was less curiosity than a sense of efficiency that prompted her to open the envelope. But it was curiosity that made her open the box. Inside was a pair of gold cufflinks. A note was folded into the satin-lined top. *To Dr. A., in appreciation of our "lunches," with affection — Jilly.*

A face sprang to mind, even as she wondered about the quotation marks. Cool. Shiny blond hair, red lipstick. Esther and her parents had been invited to dinner one night and Jilly, a pre-med student, a friend of the hostess's daughter, had been there too. Jilly had spoken like that, in quotation marks. She'd wrapped her words in innuendo in a manner that seemed to Esther to be wonderfully sophisticated.

Esther was re-reading the note when the phone rang. She jumped. It was her father, apologising. He was needed at the hospital.

The pocket could not be re-sealed.

Over her chicken, which had turned out really quite well, Esther thought about her parents, seeing them now as two halves of an oyster shell, pried open. She had no idea what lay inside. She only knew that their lives had begun long before she was born and would continue even if she were to choke to death on a chicken bone that very night.

She crumpled up the pocket from the cleaner's. The jewellery box she placed on the bedside table. Much later she heard her father come home. She waited for him to come in and check on her. When he didn't, she took the box into the bathroom and emptied its contents into the toilet. The cufflinks sank. The note swirled round and round, gathering momentum before it, too, disappeared.

Rituals

There is nothing lonelier than a Shabbat table set for one, unless perhaps a Shabbat table set for two with one person missing. This is what Fern told herself as she bowed her head and covered her face before the candles. The table was set for four, with one missing. On either side of her stood her daughters, their thin voices joining in the prayer. She was grateful for their presence; indeed, felt blessed by it.

Their Friday night dinners had begun ten years ago, when Amy was a baby. At first they'd been self-conscious about chanting the prayers; especially Fern. But she had persevered, believing that there was value in a day of rest, even if what it meant for her was a day of cooking and cleaning. But still, it gave substance and shape to their lives. In those days she even baked her own challah, though she gave that up when she suddenly lost the knack, producing a succession of braided loaves whose golden, seeded crusts were sliced to reveal a hollow core lined with raw dough. *Ha'motzi lechem min ha'aoretz*...She began buying them from the A & P.

Tonight the table was graced with flowers, also from the A & P. Rina had chosen them, a bouquet of pink carnations. There was a time when Saul would bring them home, a ritual that had begun after one of their new-parent fights about the division of labour, and she had told him, "Look, I don't want a mink coat or a BMW or a live-in Nanny. All I want is some appreciation. A box of chocolates or some flowers would do just fine!" And so another ritual had begun, flowers once a week. She loved receiving those flowers and was always, despite the circumstances, surprised. When they ceased, she began buying them for herself which always made her think of a desperately lonely fellow she'd known during her single days in Toronto. He lived in the next building with his mother and twin brother, whom he supported. He had a standing order at the neighbourhood bakery for a weekly birthday cake iced with the message: *Today's a good day.*

So she was always happy to take Rina shopping with her and let her choose the flowers even if she always chose pink.

When the blessings were finished, they kissed one another and wished each other *Shabbat Shalom*. Fern couldn't recall when that had started, but the girls insisted on it each week. And then Amy would solemnly announce: "Shabbat is a day of peace and happiness." Fern could pinpoint that one. Four years ago, when they went to services one Friday night, Amy had read it in the prayer book. She was so pleased with herself that she'd painstakingly copied it down and ever since, their Friday night dinners had begun with those words.

Fern began dishing up the salad. It occurred to her that one day a week should also be set aside for rage.

In Her Shoes

With respect to how, for so long, Doris wouldn't, and then, for so long, did — did what she did with him — I thought, and all my women friends thought, even those of us who pretended otherwise, here is one for the books. Being the kind of women we were and what we were endeavouring so hard to protect. Whereas Doris, Doris had stepped out. Doris had said bye-bye. Which is why we were ever thinking about what it was they were doing, and wondering what it would be like to be *in her shoes*. Being in them in the way being in them means, considering what they were doing. "One second, in her shoes," as Gloria said, "and afterwards you could use me to mop up the floor."

Just one second.

Whether it was fun or not, and we had no doubts on that score, she was looking *worn out*. "She practically can't walk until after four in the afternoon," as Gloria said. "Like finding herself upright, after a night of acrobatics with that guy, is the world's biggest surprise. Wave your hand in front of her face, no one's home. A ghost."

So what we wondered was, How can he enjoy that? Which is what we thought each time we saw ourselves *in her shoes*. Like any one of us would give him ever so much the better time. We'd give him something to think about. Even if we couldn't put our hearts into it, the way Doris put hers. If we did that, *watch out*.

He knew it, too. He could see it in us each time he saw us, or saw us seeing him, and our husbands saw it too. Thanks to Doris, things got steamy at home. Sweaty palms, all around. Because Doris and this man she was doing these things with, whose name I can't recall, they were our test case. They were proof of what could happen if you couldn't keep a *lid* on things.

Wet pants. Mine were always that wet. We couldn't keep our knees together, sitting, when we knew Doris was doing those things. Even if she looked half dead, she was doing them. Even if her children never spoke her name. She was doing them. And Gloria, too, if you could believe the news. Whereas what Gloria said was, "I hope Doris finds all this business worthwhile. I hope she comes to her senses, soon."

Don't Cook A Pig

We cooked a pig and fourteen people took sick. The wife said pig was wrong, we should have cooked a stallion. I looked at the stallion, and figured otherwise. Yet fourteen people took sick, eighteen if you count the brothers, so could be the wife was right. Could be she is on to something.

The fourteen people who took sick have today received a questionnaire. Where do you think we went wrong? At what point did you begin to feel sick? Is it possible that your sickness had to do with mixing pig and strong drink, plus whatever else? What was the status of your health prior to your arrival? Were our actions, once you fell ill, all that might be expected? Would you come again, and how soon?

The wife hopes the responses will be in before this weekend, since this weekend we plan an even larger party. The invitations have gone out. We've hired Ted Oliver to sing and bring his band. Ted Oliver's band is a wonderful band, the finest available. As the wife says, you can't go wrong with Ted Oliver.

The brothers are coming, that's for sure.

The pig was smoked. Maybe it was the smoke. Whatever the case, we went to considerable trouble, smoking that pig. This weekend we shall not serve smoked pig, even if it is not the same pig. We are laying cucumber sandwiches by, just in case. My wife will dance. She is an extraordinary dancer, especially when Ted Oliver sings, and I think we can assure everyone a good time. We will have hot tubs on the premises as well.

My wife figures twelve. I figure eight. We shall compromise on the tubs, just as we did on the Ted Oliver band.

Last week she tried to get the Ted Oliver band, but they were on the road. That was unfortunate because, as the wife says, last week's music was definitely not up to scratch. She hardly danced at all. Then everyone took sick.

This week the brothers will be passing out their usual leaflets.

Maybe the stallion. I'm still looking him over. But not smoked. I put my foot down there.

We hope you will join us. Actually, everyone we know is invited.

Know, too, that we have a backup plan in the event it showers.

Frankly, on this one, we are leaving no stone unturned.

Family Quarrels

Young fella came up to me. Young fella said, "Old man, you're good as dead." I said, "Young fella, be polite. What have I ever done to deserve your insults?" He said, "Father, I am your son. Father, give me a dollar." I said, "Son, go to work. Earn your dollars the same as I have mine."

This made the young fella mad. He tried to take my dollar and anything else I had. He said, "Old man, father, surrender your earthly goods, or die." He tried scattering my brains with a tire iron, but I held him off with a thick board. I got him down. I said, "Young fella, son-of-a-bitch, here is a dollar. Buy your sweetheart a present." And I dropped the dollar in his face, now that he knew who was boss.

So that is how our friendship began. It is how our friendship got off to a good start. He turned out a pretty good young fella. He found employment, started thinking about settling down, raising a family, buying himself a good piece of land. I would give him a dollar or not give him a dollar, it was all the same to me. Blood is blood. You can't fault a child every time he comes up short. "Old man," he'd say, "thank you, father, you have turned my life around." "Bless you, son," I'd say, and we'd hug up to each other like lamb against lamb.

It was then the wife popped up. We hadn't seen her in some twenty years.

"There you are," she said, "the two thugs. All this time I been wondering what happened to the pair of you. Wondering would you ever get together. Now here you are, thick as thieves on the Cross."

Then she got this cunning look in her eyes, and we could see trouble coming. We could see she had old scores to settle. What she did was take out this old dollar and flutter it up in the air. "Take it if you can," she said. "If you two snakes think you are better than me, then come and get it."

So we all three looked at each other and saw there a thousand scores never had been settled. We saw all these family skeletons rattling right there in that dollar.

We flung us all three into the battle. Him with his tire iron, me with my board, and her — to hear her tell it — with nothing but sober innocence on her side.

Don't ask me how it come out. All I know is the dust, to this day, has never settled, and everytime I rehash it I've sunk lower.

109

Opening Night

Mitsubishi, the man said. Mitsubishi. This was between acts, opening night of a miserable play. But the man kept saying Mitsubishi and peering into my eyes. Each time he said it, he drew closer. Need I say I was advancing myself? I liked the look of him. I said, What's this Mitsubishi business? Is that the only word you know? The man whispered Mitsubishi in my ear. He held my hand. He rubbed himself up against me. I did a bit of rubbing back. Mitsubishi, he said. I said, Hey, is that a car! Mitsubishi, he said. He had his arms around me. His lips were nibbling on my neck. I felt all scrambled inside.

Oh, vice-versa.

You betcha, vice-versa.

People were looking at us. I guess they thought we were old friends. Some of those looking, to speak for myself, *were* old friends.

Mitsubishi, the man said.

We were rooting around in each other. My God, how we were rooting. You're the loveliest woman in the world, the man said. What a stroke of Mitsubishi we are both here. I looked around. There were about two hundred of us. Among the women, I was the tallest. No need to tell you, in my heels, I was the tallest. Mitsubishi, the man said. Where did you get those heels? Tell me you love me, he said. He whispered that in my ear as we stood clutching each other. I wanted him to kiss my breasts. I wanted to pull up my silk top and tell him to do it. When I first had breasts, walking down the street, I wanted to raise my top to strangers and invite them to kiss my breasts.

I really wanted that.

I wanted him to.

Mitsubishi, he said. Mitsubishi yourself, I said. If I did this, I said to the man, what would you go? And I snatched up my top. I felt the cool air on my breasts. My nipples were standing up like tree trunks. They were beaming like sunsets. I'd Mitsubishi them, he said. I'd Mitsubishi the dickens out of them.

Do it! I said.

He kissed first one breast and then the other. Then started over. His hands cuddled them. I wanted my whole body to leap inside his. Mitsubishi, I said. I was suddenly tearful, out of a hearty, trembling joy.

Vice-versa. Oh, vice-versa.

My friends there had never looked happier. They were getting in a bit of Mitsubishi themselves. I could read their thoughts: Helen's out of the woods, they were thinking. Finally she is out of the woods.

We were definitely, for the minute, all of us out of the woods.

Lots and lots of vice-versa.

Between acts.

We're Mitsubishi people, the man said. *Nibble-nibble*. We've found each other. No more woods.

You betcha.

The Wedding Dress

A waiter spills a tureen of soup on the bride during a wedding dinner. As the liquid spreads across her wedding dress, the bride's radiant smile turns to a grimace. The father of the bride strikes the waiter, who falls to the floor, where he receives kicks to the abdomen and head from various members of the wedding party, including the priest and the bandleader. That night the groom is unable to perform. He locks himself in the bathroom of the honeymoon suite and weeps. The bride watches television until the last national anthem dissolves to a test pattern. The waiter lies in a hospital bed with tubes up his nose.

Ten years later, the husband and wife find themselves unemployed, victims of the arrogant economic policies of an unrepentantly conservative government voted into power by a bullied populace. Soon their cupboards are bare and their child is crying. Both the man and woman are too proud to line up for food packages at the Salvation Army. Crippled by weakness, they are almost unable to move, until the woman remembers her wedding dress, rolled up in a ball in a trunk under the bed, where it has been since their night of holy matrimony. She extracts the dress from the trunk and puts it in a pot on the stove, adding copious amounts of water. The dress disintegrates as it cooks, transforming into vermicelli-like strands, floating in a vegetable stock prepared a decade earlier.

As the family sits down at the table to eat, there is a knock at the door. It is the waiter. He has been searching for them all these years, and has come at last to apologise for his clumsiness. He wears a mask to hide his disfigured face, and his arms and torso are stiff as he enters the house. Instead of the flurry of blows he had anticipated, he receives an invitation to dinner, and being himself a hungry victim of the government of corporate interests, he accepts.

Soon the government falls, and the waiter enters the political arena, rising with unprecedented rapidity to the position of prime minister. In no time, once-abused waiters all over the world have ascended to the top positions of their respective governments. Armament factories are closed down and corporate polluters fined and jailed. No one goes without soup.

Door

Try again.

There is a closed door, and were the hall light working, one would see trails of pale scratches along its wooden surface. Presumably, a man stands before the door and try though he may, with and without the proper key, he is unable to pass through the door.

It is dark in the hallway and it is dark outside. The man peers straight up, through a skylight, and he can see only one tiny star — certainly not the moon — and its flickering presence illuminates nothing.

How tall is the man? Is the man of average height? Is he taller? Perhaps shorter?

The reason I ask is that if the man is of a sufficiently compact stature, there is nothing — short of his own lack of existence — that would prevent him from simply walking *beneath* the door. The door, you see, does not actually meet the floor at the bottom. There is a gap of perhaps three-quarters of an inch.

The man, however, may not be aware of this gap beneath the door. There is no light in the room beyond, and so the gap is not visible. If the woman in the room were to turn on a light, it would spill across the floor like a pale welcome mat. The man, not much larger than a june bug, would be attracted to this light and stroll through the opening.

But the man is crumpled in front of the door and he is exhausted from sobbing. He has been sobbing for such a long time that his eyes are dry and his throat hurts. His fingertips bleed slightly from his efforts at clawing the door open. His shoulder still aches from his attempts to batter the door down with his own body. And chances are the man is larger than a june bug.

Since it is dark, we cannot be sure, but there are statistics on this sort of thing, and these statistics can be consulted.

In the history of mankind — since the beginning of time, since the Finger of God tapped our lush, green sphere and dropped the first humans onto its fragrant surface — how many men have been the size of a june bug?

No man — no adult man — has ever been the size of a june bug. At least, no skeleton of a man this size has ever been recovered. There is no museum in the world containing such a skeleton.

In the dark, before the door, the man breathes slowly. He feels resigned, beaten, and in the dark he is beginning to question his own existence. Or at least, the value of his own existence.

He wishes the woman inside would turn on the light. And then he would know that she was there. Or that she was alive.

His lips are moving, continually moving. It is dark, and therefore impossible to see what words they are spelling out. We put our fingers to his lips and after a few repetitions, we can make out his message.

"Would god I were a june bug that I may walk beneath this door. Would god I were a june bug..."

The Squirrel

I slept in a room four feet by four feet, no doors, no windows, not even an air vent. I got there by evolving from a microscopic speck that entered through the pores in the walls.

So I slept there, I spent the night, and when I woke I was rubbing my face, rubbing the sleep from my cheeks, my chin, my eyes, and I found tracks across my face, little paw-prints—squirrel tracks. There had been a squirrel in my room the night before. A squirrel in my room.

I looked around to see if windows had formed, if crevices had opened, but my room was airtight. There were no squirrel vents, no squirrel flaps, no squirrel tunnels. A mystery such as this could only be solved by the greatest minds. Unfortunately, in such a hermetically sealed environment I had little or no contact with the greatest minds. I had only my own mind, and my own belly, and that strange tickling sensation in my belly.

And it hit me then. The squirrel could only have formed *inside* me, in my gut, and then when I slept, it crawled out my mouth or some other cavity, sniffed around, did a little exploring, and returned.

I ran my fingers lightly along the squirrel tracks on my face. I cradled my belly in my hands and revelled in the gentle tickling that came from within. I knew then that I was perfect.

Clean Plates, Clean Plates

Food was everything. Food was all there was. Food was it. We planned everything around food, we photographed every meal, we kept careful notes on every breakfast, lunch and dinner. We remembered the attempt on Reagan's life by what food we were eating when the bulletins came on. We remembered grandfather's last words by what was on the hospital meal tray in front of him at that moment. We remembered who we loved, and who we dated, and whose hearts we broke by the meals we ate on the various occasions. We talked about politics, we talked about sports, we talked about theatre and painting and film and literature, we talked about ecology and traffic congestion, but mostly we talked about food, and when we didn't we had food in front of us. During Monday's breakfast, we discussed Tuesday's dinner — would we go Italian, Indian, or try out that Lebanese place already? And when we cooked at home we spent hours at the supermarket first, finding just the right cut of this or that, and making sure the vegetables and fruits were absolutely firm, or absolutely tender, as the case may be. We asked the grocery boys questions, questions we already knew the answers to, questions that would make us feel secure, or sometimes questions that might solve something that really did puzzle us. Sometimes we copped a feel, too, if we felt so inclined. But I'm digressing, probably because I haven't eaten in days, and this is something new for me. I can feel my guts, my insides, feel the gurgle of every intestine and vein and artery and nerve that winds through my body, through my flesh, beneath my bones, around my bones, above my bones. I can feel the great, echoey, cavernous halls of my stomach, the thumping of my startled heart, the throbbing of my very brain. I can feel my hair grow, my fingernails grow, my scars heal. The funny thing was, we never cleaned the plates, the sink would fill to the brim, past the brim, with plates and cups and forks and glasses, a veritable Babel of culinary debris, and we would let it sit, the scraps of potato, the fatty edges of beef, the grains of leftover rice going through marvellous and unbelievable changes, in colour and in physical property and in smell. And when we eventually got fed up, and it did take a long time, sometimes weeks, once two months, we would either throw out the entire lot and buy huge packages of paper plates and paper cups and plastic forks and knives and spoons, or else we would hire someone, a student perhaps, and have them go through the sink, the counter, the kitchen floor, the top of the stove, the refrigerator, the table, of course, and the radiator, wherever we might have found a surface on which to heap our soiled dinnerware and cutlery. It wasn't, as some have suggested, that we were unwilling to take responsibility for our gluttony, it was just that it didn't seem necessary, it seemed a waste of time, time we could spend doing other things, and we did have activities aside from eating, though I know this probably surprises you. We worked for a living, for god's sake, how else to pay the rent, to stock the fridge, to pay the restaurant tab, to buy the theatre ticket, to pay the babysitter? Sometimes we danced, we played pool, we smoked narcotic substances, we went on gallery outings. I don't have claws, you know, and I don't own a set of dripping fangs, I don't kill my own animals, ripping their throats with my teeth. I eat a burger, I eat fish, a nice salad, baked potatoes, I eat steak, maybe wrapped in bacon, I eat a shiny, red apple, a grapefruit, a bowl of breakfast cereal. I don't kill or hunt, I have no license for such things. And so the scratches here on the wall, the long trails of paleness in the dark wood here, they are not mine, nor are the screams that you heard last night, or the blisters on my fingers, they are not mine, I take no responsibility for them, the dark rings beneath my eyes, put them on the list as well, they are not mine, they belong, presumably, to another.

Flies

Could there be anything other than the large, spindly spider perched on the ceiling of the shower stall? The steam wrenches the bastard loose, and it does a suspended waltz that sends shivers along my spine, as if I thought it could lower down and envelop me in the soft chow mein of its spider embrace.

And is there anything else to fear, anything else worth fearing? What about the waves of liquid that rush through the street, three metres high, threatening to smother, always smothering, why so much smothering? To be washed away down the street, out of the city, off the edge of the planet, and right the hell out to the stars to drift into eternity where I can finally rest, think, catch my breath in that airless vacuum. A vacuum that bangs against my door each morning, waking me up, sending me tumbling amidst a tangle of blankets to the floor, to smash away with a clenched fist at the blameless alarm clock, the alarm clock that isn't even wound up.

Let me cry, then, let my tears finally reach my shoulders from the floor, let me release that godawful flow of pain, and scream so that my voice echoes way beyond the confines of my skull, heard maybe by that astronaut, yeah, that astronaut, the one drifting without a lifeline farther and farther away from the yolk of his life. I will no longer have to beat the flies away from my head, nor beat into submission the rats that nibble eagerly at my toes.

The most little puff of smoke rises from the top of my skull. Outside the crowds are rejoicing.

The Number Six Richmond — I.

Cool prose, hot prose, take your choice. (Morning porridge of discourse: at the Richmond-Huron stop, it is definitely cool prose.) The Woman Toward Whom I Tilt My Umbrella, this lashing down cold rain day, is definitely on the left-hand side of the scale, — even more like *cold*, even more like *icy*. She looks at me with that London look "as if I was offering to bite her on the arm;" (they look at you as if you were offering to bite them on the arm, as my mother used to say.)

Then there is the Bus Driver: he, who should be extreme aridity in the word topsoil, is into demonstrating a few manoeuvres from last night's basketball game at the U. (No, his hands don't actually leave the wheel, aghast Commissioners, — but) he *can feint, dribble, pivot, pass, shoot...* and he *weaves through that defense*, spooking them with eyes and whirly hand flutters that all come from his tongue. I expect to see the oncoming lanes slide their knee-burn wheels one more time.

The crowd roars. The Bus Driver (cheer leaders) jumps up such volume that the Shift Workers open their eyes and automatically begin wiping their blurred dreams off the steamy windows. *Reality* is your stop always, so I get off the Richmond Six at Reality (though I really want to see the hoop-netting swish round the steering-wheel just one more time).

The Number Six Richmond — II.

Cool prose, hot prose, there is no choice really. Just what the pavement is now picking up (feet) from all those *Big Word Territories* layered below. I put on my see-legs, the better to lip-read them. *Territories*; past passers-by (God, how they *Talked*: talked to keep warm, blew out the cursing onto their freezing hands, shout-lashed the tired dray-horse, turning toward the Market).

"It is only an extension of your feet (the bus)," as McLuhan used to say, being the Bus Driver driving the round table where we sat; (1949, St. Mike's....O look, see Eliot intercepting that La Forgue...).

Tumbledown Taxi

It is getting pretty crowded in the Tumbledown Taxi. We sit in layers, and I marvel at the strong thighs of the sixteen-month-old baby, who is three people under me. Baby Buddha, what is weight to the weightless after all? My head/eyes point frontwards, perforce, past the large, joggling plastic puppy that The Driver has looped under his ear and then wound (stem) round his neck. Still it bobbles, joggles. There is the tumbledown taxi 'in joke' that it's time we all get out and push. (There is that tumbledown taxi pre-requisite that all front-seat passengers take the special training certificate on how to get out and be 'ready to push' every time the Driver shifts gears. The back-seat people are as yet untrained fully, but aware that they may get promoted.

There is constant coming and going as if to another planet, all pretty cheerful and with a minimum of gear. Practically one flesh, after a couple of hills, we are attuned to the needs of the second layer, and the third. I am happy with the new voluntary rotation system but not with the weight of Baby Buddha, who is now atop the B.B. Mother who is atop *me*. Rather than stop to eat: ("too much logistics," says the Driver, fiddling with his plastic poppy petals in the sideburn area), we munch/crunch/sip our singing words, beating out *Happy, Happy, Happy, Happy* on a neighbour's haunch as the Driver seems to recall it is perhaps some fêteful occasion in the life of the Tumbledown Taxi.

The Band Played Sousa

He was a high school band director who loved Sousa, but he had a wife who dominated him by her Christian forbearance, so one day he took advantage of his position and had a reckless chubby fifteen-year-old majorette up on his desk melting like vanilla ice-cream over his hand while the band outside — waiting for rehearsal to begin — broke spontaneously into *The Stars and Stripes Forever* to mock him and her, and just then a Band Parent, Mrs. Kirby — who could have been any parent, yours or mine — walked in and caught them. Mrs. Kirby was a woman who liked to put things right. His career was destroyed. He was sent to prison as an example to others and while in prison was selected to umpire a softball game between two teams of women prisoners. They played at night under the lights — so the game seemed to exist only as a series of flash photographs. There were no spectators. Both teams were nude. The girls were not all pretty — many were scrawny, with bad teeth and crooked limbs — but virtually all of them were tattooed. The most spectacular woman played first base for one of the teams; she had the outline of a panther tattooed across her body from ankle to wrist. Every move was a pounce.

   After the game was over they killed him and buried him in a corner of the exercise yard, then turned out the lights, so, as far as anyone knows, this never happened.

Denmark

Uncle Billy Watt returned after 20 years in America and immediately acquired a garden allotment from the local authority. He planted a hedge around his plot, as the other older fellows did, and constructed a hut — as they did — but unlike them, he did not grow hefty vegetables or exotic, extravagant flowers. Instead, he created a perfectly square green lawn.

The other gardeners felt mocked and insulted — it was a shameful waste. They complained to the authorities. A query was consequently sent out to Uncle Billy and he replied that he was an artist — studying the properties of Square-ness and Green-ness — and the authorities shrugged.

But there was worse. It soon became evident that Uncle Billy was bringing women to his summer hut (likely other men's wives), and if you happened to peer by chance over his hedge almost any morning you would see the square green patch strewn with women's undergarments tossed in irregular shapes, many of them colourful. You thought of the women slopping about, loose as water.

Again there was protest, but Uncle Billy was scornful. He told the local councillors that they knew nothing about art. The garments were necessary, he said, to lift the green to the sky, to catch the eye of god, (and here he went too far), to make god grunt.

Worship

You see him at Tim Horton's — the one-time Baptist minister who was thrown out of his own church for, one day during a thunderstorm, standing in the back yard naked as the day he was born. He regrets that now, he says, a lifetime of faith lost for a moment's overwhelming passion. And he defends the committee that sent him packing. "What would happen if everybody did that?" he asks. "Next thing you know we'd be worshipping thunder."

But he's a weak vessel, Lord knows. In a moment he's ordered two Boston cremes and a Dutchie and is telling me about this woman he knows who, when she gets dressed, picks up her underpants with her toes. Isn't that amazing?

Marshall Wilby's Daughter #3

In the 10K run from St. Martin to Salmon River Beach only Marshall Wilby's daughter ran naked. There was some complaint abut it. The other competitors felt she was making an illegitimate fashion statement and she made them look dowdy, they said, and if they ran naked they'd flop, one way and another. Worse, she was being followed by a whole lot of people on bicycles, sniffing her perfume, some of them married and some of them married women.

Now Jim Birks is holding study sessions devoted to her elusive nature up at the Toyota's Dealer's showroom on Sunday afternoons and there have been complaints to the authorities again, allegations of divinity.

Uncle Harry's Truck

Uncle Harry came out of the Legion to find two naked girls sitting in his pick-up truck. He was surprised. He went back into the Legion to collect his wits and have another beer. You might think he'd already had one too many, but no, he says, they were still there when he came out again. He thought they might be getting cold so he gave them the keys to the truck so they could run the heater, then went back into the Legion for another beer, but got worried about the muffler on the truck and the girls dying of monoxide poisoning so he went back out again and they were gone. He said he wasn't going to call the police. They were real good-looking. He never saw the pick-up truck again. They were one blonde and one brunette, he says, and he could say more but not in mixed company. What he's decided is that they were country and western singers on their way to Texas to get a start and he's sticking to that. Sometimes you hear a girl duet on the radio and there, says Uncle Harry, those are the girls who stole my truck.

Contributors' Notes

Byrna Barclay lives in Regina, Saskatchewan. She is the author of the novels *Summer of the Hungry Pup* and *The Last Echo*, and a book of short stories, *From the Belly of a Flying Whale*.

Lesley Choyce teaches part-time at Dalhousie University and has over 20 adult and young adult books in print. He founded THE POTTERSFIELD PORTFOLIO and Pottersfield Press, which he runs out of a 200 year-old farm house at Lawrencetown Beach overlooking the ocean. He is considered the father of transcendental wood-splitting.

Jon Cone, originally from Ontario, currently lives in Iowa City. He is the editor of WORLD LETTER.

Beverley Daurio's most recent books are Hell *& Other Novels* (Coach House Press, 1992) and *Internal Document* (Streetcar Editions, 1992). Her short fiction has appeared in journals across Canada, including *West Coast Line*, *Rampike*, and *Prairie Fire*.

Cary Fagan is the author of *History Lessons* (fiction), *City Hall and Mrs. God: A Passionate Journey Through a Changing Toronto*, and co-editor of *Streets of Attitude: Toronto Stories*. His next collection of stories, *The Little Black Dress: Tales from France*, will be published in 1993. Cary Fagan lives in Toronto.

M.A.C. Farrant has been published in many of the literary journals in Canada, and in Australia as well. She has published three chapbooks with Berkeley Horse, and in 1991 published her first collection of short fiction, *Sick Pigeon*, which was nominated for a B.C. Book Prize and a finalist for the Commonwealth Writers Prize 1992 for First Book. She lives and writes in Sidney, B.C.

Cherie Geauvreau has published poetry and fiction in several literary journals including *CFM*, *The American Voice*, *Fireweed*, and *CV II*. She lives and writes on Saltspring Island, the centre of the universe.

Vancouver writer J.A. Hamilton has recently published work in *The New York Times* and *Seventeen* magazine. Her most recent books are *Body Rain*, a collection of poetry, and *July Nights,* a collection of short fiction, appeared in spring 1992.

Elizabeth Hay was born in Owen Sound, Ontario in 1951. She has published two books: *Crossing the Snow Line* (1989) and *The Only Snow in Havana* (1992). She lives in Ottawa.

Robert Hilles lives in Calgary with his wife Rebecca and two children, Breanne and Austin. He has published many poems in various magazines in Canada. His books of poetry include: *Look , the Lovely Animal Speaks*, *An Angel in the Works*, and *Finding the Lights On*. The works included here are from a new manuscript tentatively called *Raising of Voices*.

P.J. Holdstock came to Canada from England in 1974, and is now living in British Columbia. Her short fiction has appeared in literary journals in the UK and across Canada. She has published two novels, *The Blackbird's Song* and *The Burial Ground*, and is working on a third.

Helen Humphreys is the Toronto author of two collections of poetry; *Gods and Other Mortals* and *Nuns Looking Anxious, Listening to Radios*. Her most recent work is the novel *Ethel on Fire*.

Karl Jirgens is the author of *Strapado* (a novel collection of short stories published by Coach House Press). He has edited *Rampike* magazine since its inception in 1979. He lives in Toronto, and is currently working on a new extended fiction which will be published by Mercury Press.

Sarah Klassen, a former high school English teacher, lives and writes in Winnipeg. Her first book of poetry, *Journey to Yalta* (Turnstone Press, 1988) received the Gerald Lampert Memorial Award. Her second, *Violence and Mercy* (Netherlandic Press, 1991), was nominated for the McNally Robinson "Manitoba Book of the Year Award."

John B. Lee recently won second place in CBC Radio's Literary competition for 1991. He has many books in print, including The Black Barns Trilogy (*Rediscovered Sheep*, *The Bad Philosophy of Good Cows*, and *The Pig Dance Dreams*) and *The Hockey Player Sonnets*.

M. Anne Mitton is an educator, performer and writer who lives in Fredericton, N.B. Her work has appeared in *Descant*, *The Fiddlehead*, *Open Windows* and numerous other publications. She is currently working on a book of postcard fiction entitled *Inside Stories*.

Barbara Novak finds it increasingly precarious trying to earn a living as a writer in London, Ontario, where she is currently at work on a stage play about Alma Mahler.

Leon Rooke's *Who Do You Love?*, 26 stories, appeared in spring 1992. A 1991 volume, *The Happiness of Others,* reprinted some of his earlier stories. He has published nearly 300 stories, in addition to the novels *A Good Baby*, *Shakespeare's Dog*, and *Fat Woman*.

Stuart Ross is a Toronto author whose work has appeared both in numerous chapbooks such as *In This World* (Berkeley Horse) and *Paralysis Beach* (Pink Dog Press) and in literary magazines across the country, such as *Rampike, Paragraph, WHAT!, 1cent newsnotes,* and *Industrial Sabotage.*

Colleen Thibaudeau lives and writes in London, Ontario. She is the author of *The Martha Landscapes.*

Kent Thompson is a fiction writer, actor, playwright, teacher and editor in Fredericton, New Brunswick, who originated the postcard version of the very short story when he was the Canadian Writer-in-Residence in Scotland in 1982-83.

Kristina Russelo lives in Amherstburg, Ontario. Since 1989 she has served as an editor with Black Moss Press. When not occupied with things literary, her time is largely taken up with her work as a volunteer ambulance attendant in the town where she lives.